W9-AXF-176

# The Magic Lamp

# The Magic Lamp

by

Inis Irene Hurd

Watercolors by Ethel Gesner

Drawings by Bonnie Irvine

CHRISTIAN CENTER OF CHRISTOS WISDOM

LONG BEACH

*Frontispiece*

*In bidding him good-bye, I knew*
*Within my seeing heart*
*That we attract from nature's law*
*Our own true counterparts.*



The Christian Center of Christos Wisdom, Long Beach 90814

 Published 1989
Printed in the United States of America
97 96 95 94 93 92 91 90 5 4 3 2 1

Library of Congress Cataloging in Publication Data

Hurd, Inis Irene, 1888-1984.
The magic lamp / by Inis Irene Hurd ; watercolors by Ethel Gesner ; drawings by Bonnie Irvine.
p. cm.
Summary: With the aid of the Rainbow Fairies, the young elf Squeaky Voice pursues his quest for enlightenment, opposed by the evil Black Mara.
ISBN 0-944517-00-5 (alk. paper)
[1. Fantasy. 2. Stories in rhyme.] I. Gesner, Ethel, ill. II. Irvine, Bonnie, ill. III. Title.
PZ8.3.H94Mag 1989
[Fic]--dc19 87-30728
CIP
AC

# Contents

# Acknowledgments

We gratefully acknowledge those who contributed to the publication of this edition: Ethel Gesner, who expressed the vision of this story in beautiful watercolors; Bonnie Irvine, whose fresh drawings enliven the text pages; Elizabeth Grant Fiala, who provided manuscripts, and contributed materials to support the typography; Mark Mulholland, who configured the desktop publishing system and gave insight into technical concerns; Mary Laskin, who assisted in obtaining the publishing system; and Joanne Kropacek, who handled the transfer of copyright. We are especially indebted to Mary Louise Crocker, whose generosity supported the printing of this edition, and whose good sense and good taste guided its preparation.

JANET TRONE
EDITOR

# Introduction

*The Magic Lamp* is an adventure tale in verse. For readers who wish to understand its allegory, the following notes are provided:

| | |
|---|---|
| Queen Fairy, or Dawn | *the awakener of conscious mind* |
| Squeaky Voice | *the tiny, groping human spark, seeking evolution, light, and truth* |
| Grandad Elf, or Red Baw | *the Wisdom of the Ages, who counsels the human soul in cosmic truth* |
| Golden Fay | *intuition, or conscience* |
| Black Mara | *Satan, or the Devil* |
| Shadow Moat | *the Land of Fear, surrounding Mara's place* |

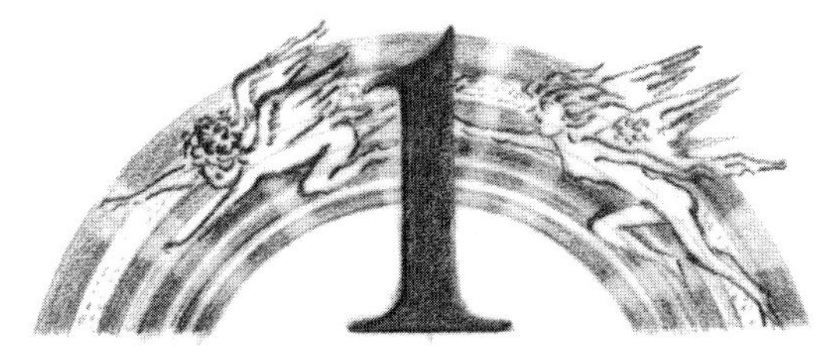

## THE RAINBOW FAIRIES AND THE SUNBEAMS

I come to introduce myself
And all my nature friends,
To prove to you the reason why
True magic never ends.
I am the queen of Fairyland.
We fairies work and play
And dance with you in golden beams
Upon your water spray.

My dress is made from magic cloth
And radiates pure light;
It has all colors in its sheen,
But you would call it white.
My rainbow helpers always dress
In every shade and hue.
We take our morning beauty bath
In perfumed lilac dew.

When Winter sits upon his throne,
Surrounded by his ice,
Our fire god Agni draws our bath
And makes it warm and nice.
To prove my stories are quite true,
Please come and go with me
And travel in our nature-world,
Where magic deeds you'll see.

I'll show you how a mighty king,
Whose heart was true and brave,
Was forced to fight against his will
A wicked, evil knave.
You'll laugh the way a tiny elf
Outwitted this bad scamp
Who planned to steal from this fine king
His jeweled Magic Lamp.

You know this king as well as we,
So try to guess his name.
Our clues will tell you who he is,
This king of cosmic fame.
Some mornings he comes in your house;
Or else his children do—
Some bring the light so you can see,
And some awaken you.

Until you guess just who they are,
No faces will you see
But black interrogation points
Where faces ought to be.
Sometimes you cannot see this king,
But you can see his smiles
Across the sky, on earth and sea;
They spread for miles and miles.

This king rides 'round and 'round our earth,
And when the sky grows dark,
His queen and children ride with him
And think it quite a lark.
He cares not if your skin is black
Or yellow, brown or white,
Or whether you are rich or poor;
He shares with you his light.

He makes your sleeping dad get up,
Your mother start to cook,
The fisherman begin to fish
By baiting up his hook.
Your folks obey this mighty king
Regardless of their age.
They could not tell what time it was
Without this beaming sage.

He taught earth-folk to tell the time
Without a watch or clock.
I'll tell you how it can be done
With stick or tree or rock.
When you have solved this riddle true,
Just look upon the ground
And see his shadow short or tall,
Though he is fat and round.

The shortest shadow that he makes
Is when you lunch at noon.
His children watch you while you eat
With knife or fork or spoon.
They want to see if you are taught
To be polite and munch
(They never chew with open mouths
Or eat with noisy crunch).

They think you children impolite
When food falls from your lips.
They chew their food with mouths quite closed
And drink their milk in sips.
These children love to hide from you
And tease you with their jokes.
They laugh and play them on your pets
And sometimes on your folks.

They chase old Winter out of bed
And melt his quilt of snow.
They love to warm good Mother Earth
And make her children grow.
They watch you hang your laundry out,
Then play a joke on you—
They draw the color from your clothes
(So watch your pink and blue).

They call this joke a color one;
Your mother calls it "fade."
They laugh when she hangs colored clothes
Beneath protecting shade.
Now listen to our finest clue:
These children are called *Beams*.
They always tease your sleeping pets
And chase them in their dreams.

When pets do whimper, jump, or squirm,
These Beams are sure around.
They tweak their whiskers, nose, or ears,
And laugh without a sound.
They call to you, "Come out, come out,
And breathe some good fresh air.
Or, we'll come in and sit with you
Without a door or chair."

And then they do this very thing!
You'll see these children pass
Right through your door or windowpane
But see no broken glass.
Now guess what children need no door
To come into your house?
They come in quieter than you
Or even Mama Mouse.

They tickle you upon your face,
And if you are asleep,
They tiptoe right across your bed;
Then up your wall they creep.
When Winter lights his weather-pipe
And blows out clouds of smoke,

These Beams play hide and seek with you
And think it quite a joke.

Old Winter cannot stop this king
From smiling on our earth.
He heals the sick and chases gloom
And chuckles in his mirth.
At last you guessed my riddle true:
The Sunbeams and King Sun!
Of course you like their teasing jokes,
And play with them is fun.

These Sunbeams played a joke on us,
Then ran away and hid.
I fear we fairies were to blame;
I'll tell you what we did.
We went with them right after school,
To ride across the sky.
Our rainbow was a lovely one,
Quite bright and very high.

"Come to our milk-house," said the Beams,
"And watch our milkmaids work.
We Sunbeams play, but not these maids—
They never think to shirk."
We fairies saw great pans of cream,
And milkmaids clean and neat.
The Sunbeams said, "Please make ice cream,
And make it nice and sweet."

"Be seated, then," a maid replied
But tossed her saucy head.
"You should not eat such rich ice cream,
But wholesome milk and bread."
The maids froze ice cream shaped like stars,
And cups of custard whey,
And then—they poured the skimmed milk out
Upon the Milky Way!

We fairies gasped, "You're wasting milk!
Is that the reason why
The Milky Way is always white
Against the evening sky?"
The Beams replied, "We waste no milk.
We love to serve our friends,
And feed our baby stars warm milk—
On milk their life depends.

"Our Milky Way belongs to them.
Go look, and you will see
A nursery full of baby stars
As healthy as can be."
We talked and waited for our treat,
And when the cream was made,
We ate beneath the Wisdom Tree,
Protected by its shade.

The Sunbeams said, "Please serve our friends.
Queen Fairy is our guest.
Serve her and then her fairy friends

The choicest and the best."
The Sunbeams ate the custard whey;
We ate the ice-cream stars.
They laughed and said, "We use sour milk
To diet sad, old Mars."

"And who is Mars?" I asked the Beams—
A guest must be polite;
The ice cream was too rich, but then,
So was our appetite.
"Old Mars," they said, "is god of war,

And just because of that,
He gets no ice cream or sweet milk.
Besides, he is too fat.

"His rule is honest but severe;
His sadness makes him stern.
He feels disgraced because his son
Would not obey or learn.
His son was Mara, and he grew
More evil every year.
His bold exploits enticed our youth;
Our realm began to fear.

"He would not learn our cosmic law!
The truth just made him worse.
He planned to rule our Father Sun
And all our universe.
Old Mars fought Mara and his plan
And warned his evil son,
'Our realm will fight for truth and light.
This battle will be won!'

"Old Mars threw Mara from our realm.
He fell to earth through space.
He is Black Mara, and he preys
Upon the human race.
His satellites went down with him,
For they were evil youth.
'We go with Mara,' they called out.
'We hate your cosmic truth.'

"They hide behind dark Shadow Moat.
They are a den of thieves.
Black Mara laughs and tricks mankind;
Earth-children he deceives.
Earth-folk call him the Evil One;
His heart is black and vile.
We Sunbeams make Black Mara run.
Our light he does defile."

"I . . . am . . . afraid . . . ," Pink Fairy sobbed—
She is so young and shy—
But when the Sunbeams served more cream,

She soon forgot to cry.
"Black Mara has to learn," I said,
"The truth of cosmic plan;
Learn how to share and not deceive,
But help, his brother man."

We talked about Black Mara's greed
And how he preyed on men,
Until the maids brought more ice cream
And served us all again.
I thanked the Sunbeams for the cream,
Although too rich and sweet.
But ice cream is a healthy food
Unless you overeat.

And that is what we fairies did,
We saw to our surprise.
We know it's better to eat less
Than to eat with greedy eyes.
But when we took our third ice cream,
Our tummies turned and said,
"Stop cramming us—we'll make you sick
And send you right to bed.

"When you cram us so full and tight,
We hurt with every touch.
You know one helping is enough—
Why do you eat so much?"
We fairies never waste our food,
So finished what we had.

By then we did not feel so good;
We really felt quite bad!

We know our tummies told the truth
About our getting sick.
And then these Sunbeams played on us
Their final laughing trick.
"Just take this castor oil," they said.
"Its flavor is so nice."
Our noses took a whiff, then said,
"Hmmm . . . lemon, clove, and spice.

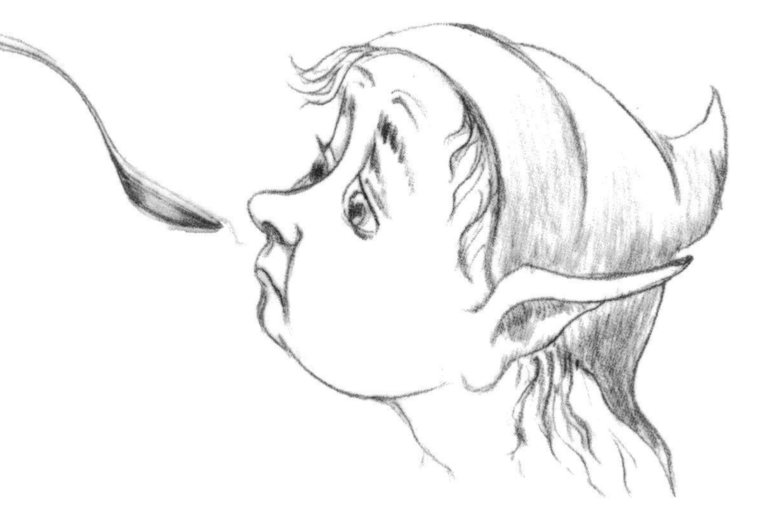

"Why do you tummies always fight
And turn and gripe and fuss?

Why be so squeamish? Drink it down.
It smells all right to us."
Our tummies answered back and said,
"You noses are too pert!
How could you know the way we feel?
When crammed too full, we hurt.

"You noses mind your business, please.
Your business is to smell.
We tummies have to digest food
To keep our children well."
Our noses turned up in the air,
Quite snooty, if you please.
We fairies knew that castor oil
Was not from lemon trees.

Our tummies groaned, "Oh, do come home
Before the close of day.
You know when children overeat,
We tummies have to pay."
I thanked the Sunbeams for their treat.
They laughed aloud and said,
"Our castor oil will make you well
And keep you out of bed."

Pink Fairy saw the Sunbeams laugh
While waving us good-bye.
She looked at them in quick distrust.
Quite watchful was her eye.
"Come, baby dear," I said to her.
"You really do look pale."
We stepped within our crescent moon
And homeward set the sail.

We were ashamed as we went home,
Too sick to fly or ride,
And sorry that we overate
And lost our fairy-pride.
The Sunbeams are quite dear to us,
The warmest of our friends;
We know King Sun gives life to earth—
On him our life depends.

Our Sunbeam friends have secret faults
I think I should expose.
When angry, they can sunburn you
Right on your saucy nose.
"Your tempers," we call out to them,
"Are really a disgrace."
And then our Sunbeams are ashamed
To burn your hands or face.

They call to us to come and play.
We let them beg awhile,
For well we know we can't resist
A Sunbeam's warming smile.
At vespers when we say our prayers,
They promise, so demure,
To keep their tempers when they play—
But we are not so sure.

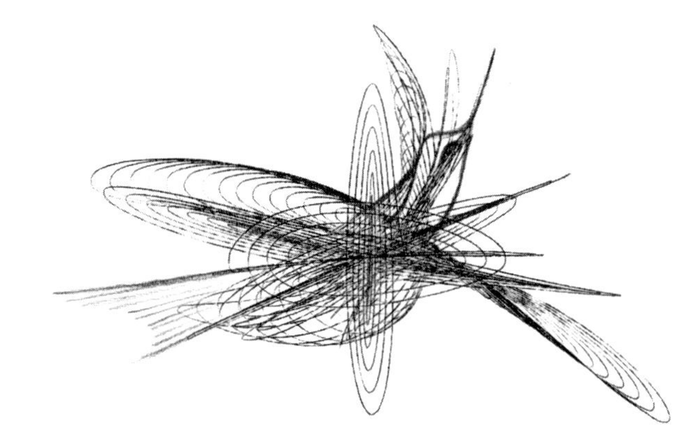

*"Our Milky Way belongs to them.*
*Go look, and you will see*
*A nursery full of baby stars*
*As healthy as can be."*

## QUEEN FAIRY MEETS YOUNG SQUEAKY VOICE AND HANDSOME SCATTER WIND

Although I am the fairy queen,
  I have my problems too.
To solve them, I just go to work
  And think each problem through.
Before our visit with the Beams,
  My fairies loved to play
On rainbows touching Mother Earth,
  But now . . . they fly away.

I asked my fairies what they feared.
  Pink Fairy sobbed and said,
"Black Mara might climb on our bow
  And snatch us out of bed."
Her fear told me what I must do—
  I started on my way
To learn about Black Mara's den
  Before the close of day.

I earthward flew where I could see,
  Beyond a garden wall,
And there upon the shady side
  There lay a bright red ball.
"I'll rest awhile," I said aloud,
  Just talking to myself.
And then this ball began to move.
  Was it a gnome or elf?

All elves wear bright red, pointed caps,
  Their coats a darker red.
They use their shoes with rolled-up toes
  To make a house or bed.
When elves remove their magic shoes,
  The left turns upside down
And fits its top into the right.
  These useful shoes are brown.

And then—you'd see the cutest house,
Complete with floor and roof.
And in this house the elves can sleep
(Their shoes are waterproof).
Their caps and coats are lined with brown,
And when they play and hide,
They turn their red clothes inside out
And wear the brown outside.

And then you see no red at all;
They look just like the ground.
And when you children call them "clods,"
They laugh without a sound.
But when you children disobey
Or talk back to your folks,
These elves become too sad to laugh
At any of your jokes.

I thought about this sleeping elf,
Then tickled his pert nose.
He startled when he heard my wings
As quickly I arose.
He rubbed his eyes and yawned and yawned
And jumped up from his nap.
I said, "I am the fairy queen."
He doffed his bright red cap.

This elf replied, "I'm Squeaky Voice.
My grandad is Red Baw.
He teaches cosmic truth and light
In Mother Nature's law."
I liked this elf—he was well trained,
And he had truthful eyes.
"Where are your parents?" I asked him.
He answered with surprise.

"They travel with my granny elf
To teach this cosmic plan:
All life is *ONE* in nature's law,
In ant or tree or man."
I saw this elf was very wise
And wondered if he knew
About Black Mara and his men.
This elf would answer true.

"I'm glad to meet you," I replied.
"I need some help, my lad.
My fairies fear to play on earth—
It makes them very sad.
When calling on our Sunbeam friends,
They told a tale to me
About a giant on the earth,
As evil as can be.

"His name is Mara, and I'm told
He lives not far from here.
Earth-folk call him the Evil One.
He rules through greed and fear."
Young Squeaky said, "We elves know him
And hate his evil ways.

My grandad says that selfish men
Enjoy his fawning praise."

I saw the garden summer-dry,
And rising heat-waves float.
Young Squeaky said, "It is so hot—
May I remove my coat?"
Before I could reply, we heard
A terrifying sound.
We saw, as pistol shots rang out,
Brown bullets hit the ground!

A cracking, popping, zipping noise
Now sounded by our side.
We looked around for any place
Where we could safely hide.
Of course, I could have flown away,
Which would have been unjust—
Young Squeaky was protecting me
With elfin pride and trust.

We hid beneath a pumpkin leaf.
The shots came fast and loud.
This tiny elf was not afraid
But stood quite poised and proud.
Hard bullets fell upon our leaf,
Then bounced upon the sod.
I saw a Beanstalk cradle-swing
Her dancing baby pod.

It swayed upon its parent stem,
Who laughed and tossed it high
Among the Beanstalks twisted tight,
All summer-cured and dry.
"Who shot at us?" I asked the Bean,
But when no answer came,
I called aloud, "It cannot *be*—
Your children are to blame?"

The Beanstalk laughed, "Who *shot* at you?"
Then said in joyous mirth,
"The heat released my children Beans
To feed good Mother Earth.
Besides, my children are well trained—
They grow all summer long.
You heard them shouting their good-byes,
For they are plump and strong.

"That cracking, popping, zipping sound,
That terrifying noise,
Was made by drying, bursting pods
And not by naughty boys.
My Beans call out from bursting pods,
'At last we Beans are free
To ride and dance with Scatter Wind!
What wonders we shall see!'

"Next spring my children Beans will grow
Their Beanstalks tall and green,
And when matured, each pod will burst

To free a handsome Bean.
So let them dance and shout and play,
For soon they sleep and rest
Beneath old Winter's soft white snow—
A tribute to their quest."

The ripened Corn began to laugh;
Her gossip ears were wide.
The Pumpkin gaped like dullard folk
Inane with foolish pride.
The Pumpkins thought themselves quite choice
Because the Corn had said,
"My listening ears keep me informed.
I am no 'pumpkin head'!"

Young Scatter Wind now jumped across
The grapevine garden wall.
Old Beanstalk warned us he was there
With friendly, knowing call.
She whispered low, "Come, fairy queen,
Come hide inside this pod.
Young Scatter Wind has work to do,"
She laughed with artful nod.

"He waits until our summer goes
And then comes breezing 'round.
He mixes seeds and scatters them
Upon our waiting ground.
Our garden maidens flirt with him—
He's handsome and quite strong.

Tonight we hold our garden dance
And sing our harvest song."

*"He waits until our summer goes*
*And then comes breezing 'round.*
*He mixes seeds and scatters them*
*Upon our waiting ground."*

As Squeaky Voice climbed in the pod,
Beside the fairy queen,
He did not know that Scatter Wind
Their hiding place had seen.
Young Scatter Wind began to sing
As to himself he thought,
"I've longed to meet the fairy queen.
Her favor I have sought.

"I tipped my hat to her one day
As she was flying past.
I heard her tell her fairy friends
I was too rough and fast.
This is my chance to win from her
A thank-you and a smile.
(Although I am a gentleman,
A female cramps my style.)

"I do not know that solemn elf,
Although I've seen his face.
But if he is Queen Fairy's friend,
I'd better check my pace.
I'll show that elf King Sun's fine home,
A ride he can't resist."
He blew the pod from parent-stem
With quick and mighty twist.

The bean pod spiraled as it sailed
Up in the evening sky.
Young Scatter Wind called, blithe and gay,
"Hold on, we're sailing high!"
All lovelorn swains are just alike
When courting maidens fair:
Their heads become vacuums
Beneath their shining, well-groomed hair.

Then softly sang young Scatter Wind,
"O gracious fairy queen,
You are the sweetest sprite of all,
The fairest ever seen.
I've waited long, O lovely one,
For you to ride with me—
The beauty of King Sun's fine home
Is something you should see.

"Too bad we had to bring this elf.
But since he is along,
Tell him to be our radio
And sing an elfin song."
Embarrassed little Squeaky Voice
For once forgot to squeak.
"Come, Scatter Wind," he firmly said,
"This ride we did not seek.

"Queen Fairy is your guest and friend
And has the right, good sir,
To recognize a gentleman
Before he speaks to her.
You were not introduced to her;
Your manners are quite rude.

Within her realm you would not dare
  Your presence to intrude."

I was amazed at Squeaky Voice.
  He really was quite wise.
Young Scatter Wind began to flush,
  So great was his surprise.
He straightened out our sailing pod,
  Then roguishly replied,
"The beauty of our fairy queen
  Could never be denied."

He laughed at Squeaky's sober face,
  Then turned to me and said,
"Forgive my admiration, please.
  Your presence turns my head.
Who introduced this elf to you?
  If I may please inquire.
He is quite brave to censure me.
  His courage I admire."

"I am the fairy queen," I said.
  "I introduce myself.
And I present young Squeaky Voice,
  A wise and honest elf."
Young Scatter Wind and Squeaky Voice,
  In deference to me,
Returned each other's bows, then grinned,
  As friendly as could be.

I told about Black Mara, and
  My rainbow fairies' plight.
"I know him," Scatter Wind replied.
  "He hates the truth and light.
Please do not fear, for I will see
  What he intends to do.
He hates the spirit of our wind—
  Our realm he does eschew.

"Let Squeaky see King Sun's fine home
  Before the close of day—
The planets and the sapphire stars
  And then the Milky Way."
"I can't accept," said Squeaky Voice,
  "To take this wondrous ride
Unless our fairy queen consents.
  We must let her decide."

"I've seen King Sun's fine home," I said,
  "But gladly give consent
For Squeaky Voice to take this ride.
  Our time will be well spent."
With joy young Squeaky gasped aloud,
  Then sat in speechless awe.
Through rainbow arches we could see
  The home of cosmic law.

Tall golden towers then appeared,
  And slowly one by one
They formed a circle to protect

*The bean pod spiraled as it sailed*
*Up in the evening sky.*
*Young Scatter Wind called, blithe and gay,*
*"Hold on, we're sailing high!"*

The home of wise King Sun.
This auric splendor now enclosed
Within a crystal dome
The Magic Lamp of truth and light,
The jewel in each home.

White diamonds and sapphire stars
Outlined this dome so rare.
(The evening sky reflected true
Its jewels shining there.)
This dome was crowned with rubies red
And emeralds of green.
Their colors sparkle when King Sun
Pays homage to his queen.

She guides the growth of baby stars
With gentle, kindly ways.
Her lullabies are filled with light,
For they are songs of praise.
Deep silence reigned in all the spheres—
The time had come to rest.
In awe we glided back to earth,
All gone our laughing zest.

To win true friends, you must possess
A friendly heart and mind.
True friendship comes in many forms,
And Scatter Wind was kind.
He smiled and stopped our bean-pod craft,
Then laughed and helped me down.
In laughter he would clothe defeat,
But never in a frown.

In bidding him good-bye, I knew
Within my seeing heart

That we attract from nature's law
  Our own true counterparts.
Young Squeaky thanked me for the ride,
  Then grinned in quick delight,
For Scatter Wind had disappeared
  Within the silent night.

I smiled when Squeaky bowed and said,
  "Tell Scatter Wind good-bye—
I see he waits to take you home
  Since both of you can fly."
I bade good-bye to Squeaky Voice
  But laughed within myself—
Young Scatter Wind was not so wise:
  He had not fooled this elf.

EHG

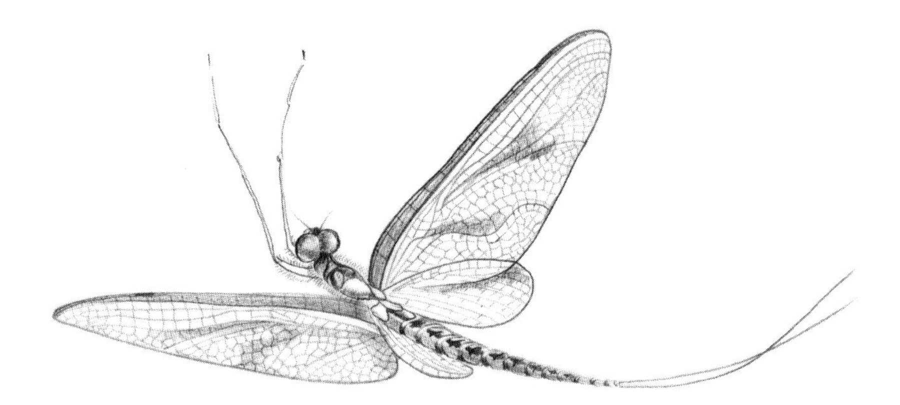

*We hid beneath a pumpkin leaf.*
*The shots came fast and loud.*
*This tiny elf was not afraid*
*But stood quite poised and proud.*

## SQUEAKY VOICE MEETS BLACK MARA

"Good-bye, good-bye," called Squeaky Voice
To the lovely fairy queen;
He heard the echo of her laugh,
But she could not be seen.
Then homeward little Squeaky went.
His mind was thinking fast.
The garden Beans looked up and grinned
As he went running past.

He must find out where Mara lived!
Queen Fairy should be free
To play on rainbows touching earth
As well as sky and sea.
He knew Black Mara was called "black,"
But not because of race—
His *heart* was black with evil deeds,
But white his cruel face.

Black magic was the art he used
To buy the soul of man;
He laughed when children disobeyed
And scoffed at cosmic plan.
"Good souls fear Mara," Squeaky thought,
"Be they of man or sprite."
Then Squeaky saw deep in the woods
The flicker of a light.

He crept quite close and saw some men:
Each wore a robber's mask.
They bragged about their stolen loot
While drinking from a flask.
Then Squeaky heard with great surprise
The leader slyly say,
"I'll carry Mara's box to him.
Too bad we had to pay."

"It served its purpose very well,"
Said one who was quite bold.
"While you were buying Mara's hat,
I robbed the store of gold."
"Come, men, and even up our load,"
The weary leader said.
"Sort out our loot—'tis time to go;
We all want food and bed."

They put Black Mara's hatbox down
Beside a giant tree.
Young Squeaky grinned as he crept 'round,
Black Mara's box to see.
"This box is pasteboard," Squeaky thought,
"And has a broken lid."
And when he saw the corner off,
He climbed right in and hid.

As soon as Mara's men were packed,
The leader called, "Let's go."
So Squeaky rode in Mara's box,
To where? He did not know.

One thing he knew, this box was safe—
From paper it was made;
Young Squeaky peeked from broken lid,
So he was not afraid.

No elf will climb inside a box
To play or try to hide;
If it can lock or close up tight,
Elves wisely stay outside.
This goes for empty houses too,
Or closets anywhere:
They will not hide in any place
That closes out the air.

They *never, never* climb inside
Of things that lock or snap:
You might get in and not get out!
Closed places are a trap.
As Squeaky rode, he heard one man
Send forth a secret call;
"We near old Shadow Moat," he said,
"I see the ocean wall."

At last they stopped and called again.
None dared to laugh or speak.
Then Squeaky heard a drawbridge drop
With dull and heavy creak.
In silence, Mara's men tramped on
Without a laugh or word.

One knocked upon a secret door.
A strong, deep voice was heard.

"Come in, you're late," the voice called out.
"Come drop your stuff down here.
Hand me that box and close that door."
The leader shook with fear.
"Look, Mara," said one whining man,
"We've brought much gold to you."
When Squeaky felt the box put down,
He knew what he must do.

He peeked outside and saw the men
Were busy pouring gold.
Black Mara gloated as he watched;
His greedy eyes were bold.
Outside the box young Squeaky dropped,
On stolen loot piled high.
He quickly hid above the door
And heaved a waiting sigh.

As he prepared to hear the plans
Of this most evil knave,
He did not know that he would be
An elfin hero brave.
He knew Queen Fairy needed help,
So came with Mara's men.
But now he saw that he had found
Black Mara's secret den.

Then Squeaky's eyes grew round and wide.
He heard Black Mara say,
"I plan to buy all honest men
Before another day."
"We're tired and hungry," one man said;
Black Mara struck him down.
"I give the orders here," he roared,
And cursed with maddened frown.

"Go call our chemist, old One Eye;
Then all of you may go.
Tell him to bring my council staff.
My plans they now must know."
Old One Eye brought the council staff,
And to them Mara said,
"We have some planning we must do
Before we go to bed.

"We have enough of gold to buy
Each greedy, selfish man;
But for the honest men of earth,
We need another plan."
Old One Eye said, "Most honest men
Will worship truth and light;
The thing to do is take away
The *power* of their might."

"Their power lies within the light,"
Black Mara then replied,
"The very light that we refused
And all of us denied.
This light comes from the Magic Lamp
Within King Sun's great home,
Where golden towers guard it well
Around its crystal dome.

"We'll steal this Magic Lamp from him
And darken cosmic space;
Then I will rule the sky and earth
And all the human race.
When men get light, they learn to think;

And that must never be.
When I possess that Magic Lamp,
All men will worship me."

Young Squeaky thought, "He has no soul.
He *is* the Evil One.
He must not steal the Magic Lamp
Away from wise King Sun!"
Young Squeaky gasped as Mara said,
"You men will not deny
My many forms deceive mankind,
Whose truth I do defy."

This was too much for Squeaky Voice;
For he and nature's youth
Were taught by Baw, his grandad elf,
To worship light and truth.
Young Squeaky whistled sharp and clear:
The startled men sat still.
And then they heard right in the room
A voice quite high and shrill.

"Who wants to worship fear and hate?"
Called little Squeaky Voice.
"Just those who sell their souls to you—
They have no other choice."
Black Mara roared, "What's that, what's that?"
And wildly looked around.
But Squeaky Voice, our tiny elf,
Was nowhere to be found.

"I'm not below," called Squeaky Voice.
"I'm here above your door!"
When Mara saw him sitting there,
He stamped upon the floor.
"Get out of here," he called aloud,
"You snooping, spying imp.
When I find out who let you in,
I'll give his hide a crimp."

"Then crimp yourself," said Squeaky Voice.
"I rode upon your hat.
And I run faster than your men—
I'm here to tell you that.
Besides, we elves know what you are.
We want no stolen wealth.
We work for everything we need,
Enjoying fun and health."

This made Black Mara fume and rage.
He called his spies to him,
"Just drop this imp in Shadow Moat
And see he doesn't swim."
But Squeaky Voice dropped to the floor,
And 'round the room he ran.
He tripped the men and called to them,
"Just catch me if you can!"

The men grew weary, then declared,
"How can this elf hurt us?
We are your wisest fighting men.

Stop making such a fuss.
To get that cosmic Magic Lamp,
We'd better start to plan.
You know King Sun brings living light
To planet earth—and man."

Young Squeaky laughed, "You have no oil,
But only gold and pelf.
That lamp would be no good to you
Just sitting on your shelf.
That lamp would never burn for you—
It burns a magic oil—
And you would add an empty lamp
To all your other spoil."

Then Squeaky Voice just disappeared
Before their very eyes.
He left confused and angry men.
Black Mara called his spies.
"Go watch King Sun as he rides north
And note the time of year.
My magic will protect you, men;
Go now and have no fear.

"Come, One Eye," Mara said to him,
"Don't sit there in a frown.
Can you make oil like old King Sun's?
Your wisdom is renowned."
Old One Eye said, "I'll make your oil
If you will bring to me

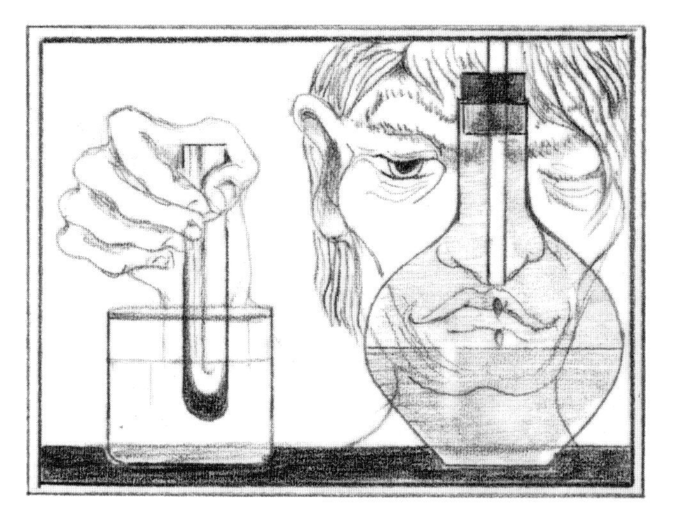

The Magic Lamp of wise King Sun:
Its power I must see."

Black Mara said, "King Sun has guards,
And one is quite confused.
He is the one that I can buy;
His knowledge can be used.
It's easy to beguile most men
Through tricks and sly deceit.
The way I make the greedy fall
Is through their own conceit.

"When earth-men have no inner sight,
They see through greedy eye;
But not the honest men of earth—

My power *they* deny."
As Mara thought about good men,
His face grew vile with hate.
If he could get the Magic Lamp,
He would decree their fate.

"Be off, you runners," he called out.
"Be ready, spies, to go;
Learn all about that special oil.
Its secret I must know."
Black Mara did not know that he,
This vile and cunning scamp,
Would burn the oil of wise King Sun—
And *in* the Magic Lamp.

The runners left dark Shadow Moat
To spy on wise King Sun.
None knew that Squeaky Voice went too,
Until they tried to run.
Then Squeaky ran between their feet
And tripped them in a sprawl.
The men found out they could not run;
Young Squeaky made them fall.

"That's Squeaky Voice," said one who knew,
For he had once been good;
But now he lived a life of crime
In Mara's darkened wood.
Young Squeaky called, "King Sun is wise;
His cosmic law is true,
Or he would never share his light
With evil men like you.

"Why don't you leave Black Mara now?
You have a chance right here."
One man struck out at Squeaky Voice
But saw him disappear.
Young Squeaky ran to tell his news
To Grandad, wise and kind,
Whose true name was Red Baw because
He had a master mind.

The name *Red Baw* still clung to him—
His hair had once been red—
But Squeaky saw long curls of white
On Grandad's hoary head.
Red Baw, his grandad, knew the way
To fight this evil one
Who was Black Mara, and who feared
The light of wise King Sun.

This light gives life to planet earth,
A magnet for her own,
Where sprite or man must reap alike
The harvest each has sown.
Young Squeaky ran in deepest thought,
His pointed cap awry.
His coattails waved to all the trees
As he went running by.

At last he reached his grandad's home,
In forest cool and sweet.
"Wake up, Grandad," he called to him,
But Grandad feigned his sleep.
"You're teasing me," said Squeaky, as
He tweaked his grandad's ear.
"I bring you news from Shadow Moat—
It's something you must hear."

"That moat surrounds Black Mara's place,"
Said Grandad in dismay.
"The ocean fills old Shadow Moat
A hundred miles away."
As Grandad heard young Squeaky's news,
He said, "We must make haste.
I'll call a council-meet tonight.
We have no time to waste.

"When children hear things that are wrong
Or see things that are bad,
They should run home and tell their folks
The way you have, my lad.
Come, Squeaky Voice, the time has come
For you to understand
How nature gods work with King Sun
To rule our magic land.

"I know that you will see strange sights
In sky and sea and ground,
But never fear if you can hear
A singing, humming sound.
This magic sound protects you, lad;
And when you hear this tone,
Just go to sleep and whisk away.
You will not be alone."

*Outside the box young Squeaky dropped,*
*On stolen loot piled high.*
*He quickly hid above the door*
*And heaved a waiting sigh.*

## MOTHER EARTH AND EARTH GOD GO APPEAR IN THE SILVER GLADE, AND SQUEAKY VOICE MEETS A MAGIC SERPENT

As Grandad Elf led Squeaky Voice
  Through deep and darkened wood,
He gave a magic call to those
  Who knew and understood.
"I've never seen a council-meet,"
  Young Squeaky whispered low.
"How can I be as wise as you
  And learn the things you know?"

"Learn how to listen," Grandad said,
  "And me, your Baw, obey.
Use well your ears and eyes, for you
  Will be White Baw someday.
Refrain from hurtful gossip, lad,
  And gain your own respect—
A lesson good for old or young,
  But one we most neglect."

"Do I mind you?" asked Squeaky Voice.
  But Grandad gently said,
"True wisdom, lad, comes from your heart.
  Its door is in your head."
"I have no door inside my head,"
  Laughed Squeaky, quite amused.
"Your door is open," Grandad said.
  "Your thinking is confused."

"What door have I inside my head?"
  Thought Squeaky to himself;
He ran and turned some somersaults,
  This honest, thinking elf.
"He seeks the answer," Grandad thought
  While watching Squeaky turn.
"Let children think their problems out—
  In solving them, they learn."

To say these somersaults had failed
Would really not be fair:
The answer came to Squeaky Voice
While turning in the air.
Instead of landing as before,
Upon his elfin feet,
He lost his balance in midair
And landed on his seat.

He jumped up, laughing, as he said,
"I know what door you mean—
It is *my mind that thinks my thoughts!*
I wonder if they're seen?"
"We see your thoughts in all your deeds,"
Said Grandad with a grin.
"Good thoughts will make you do good deeds;
Bad thoughts will make you sin."

Then Grandad and young Squeaky heard
A singing, humming tone.
Old grandad said, "Our help is near—
We travel not alone."
Then Squeaky saw, for his first time,
All kinds of nature sprites—
Some came by instinct through the woods;
Some carried colored lights.

They came from water, earth, and fire;
The winged ones, through the air
(Some flew so fast they startled him!).
He saw them everywhere.
When all had reached the Silver Glade,
Young Squeaky saw with pride
That he sat on his grandad's right,
Which was his honor side.

"Could this be Grandad," Squeaky thought,
"So dignified and grim?"
All sprites addressed him as Red Baw,
For they respected him.
Red Baw called out, "Attention, sprites.
I brought my grandson here—
He brings from darkened Shadow Moat
A message filled with fear.

"This very night, Black Mara plots
To steal from our King Sun
His Magic Lamp; and we must fight
This soulless, evil one.
We must get word to wise King Sun
About Black Mara's plan.
Each group must call its nature god
To help King Sun—and man.

"Our nature gods may manifest
In human forms tonight.
They represent each race of man—
Black, yellow, brown, and white.
We elves belong to Mother Earth,
Not water, air, or fire;

Ethel Gesner

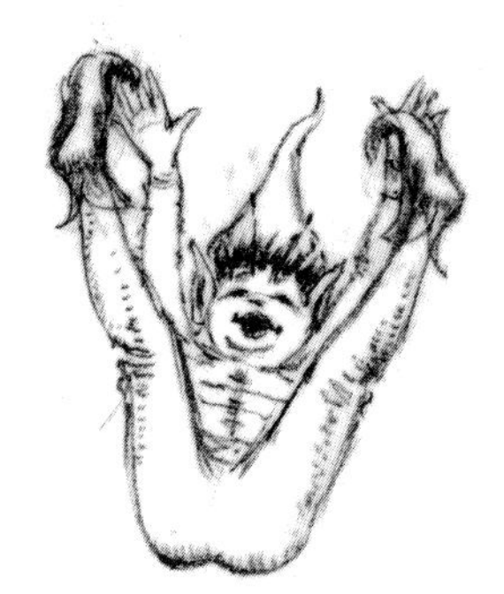

*To say these somersaults had failed*
*Would really not be fair:*
*The answer came to Squeaky Voice*
*While turning in the air.*

Come, sprites, we call upon her now.
Her counsel we desire."

The earth sprites chanted with Red Baw;
Then clearly there was heard
The blending of all nature sounds
In one long, magic word.
Rare perfume filled the Silver Glade;
And rising from the ground,
They heard, beneath the living soil,
A gentle, crooning sound.

The earth sprites clapped their elfin hands;
Then Squeaky saw appear
The lovely form of Mother Earth,
Whose eyes were keen and clear.
Her dark face beamed with growing smiles;
Her winter curls were white—
They jiggled with each step she took,
To Squeaky's great delight.

Good Mother Earth addressed Red Baw,
"I come to help defeat
Black Mara, for I heard your call
Before your council-meet.
As your earth mother, I have learned
Not to advise or speak
Until my children call to me—
My knowledge *they* must seek.

"When asking nature gods for help,
Be sure it is for *all*—
They never answer selfish pleas,
Although they hear your call.
When you climb upward on mistakes,
You soon will reach your goal;
Each upward step a golden stair,
The pathway of your soul.

"But upward, upward you must climb,
And make no downward stair.
For at its base, Black Mara waits
To laugh at your despair.
Come form a circle, nature sprites,
And sing, each grateful one.
We seek the help of earth god Go,
My young and only son."

The singing nature sprites then formed
A circle of glad hands.
They danced around good Mother Earth
To thank her seas and lands.
Then Squeaky heard that humming tone—
It sounded as before—
He felt its power lift him high,
As upward he did soar.

In dreamland, Squeaky Voice beheld
A vast and silent land.
He wondered why he stood alone.

He did not understand.
This silence frightened Squeaky Voice—
He felt the strangest fear.
He looked for Grandad or the sprites,
But not a one was near.

He saw no trees or growing things;
He heard no play or strife
Until a desert mound of sand
Moved slowly into life.

And as it opened, Squeaky saw
A serpent's head arise.
An orange flame came from its mouth.
It had no seeing eyes.

This magic serpent slowly rose
By turning 'round and 'round.
And when it stood upon its tail,
Bright flames raced on the ground.
From fear young Squeaky could not call

Nor move his rigid feet.
The flames soon covered earth and sea,
But Squeaky felt no heat.

When water could not quench the fire,
Young Squeaky plainly saw
This cosmic flame would purify
The dross of earthly law.
From flaming mouth the serpent spoke,
"Why are you not afraid?
Why don't you run away from here
And back to Silver Glade?"

"I have no power," Squeaky squeaked.
"From fear I cannot move."
The serpent said, "You answer true.
This point you had to prove.
For it is fear and only fear
That darkens truth and light.
If you can conquer fear, my lad,
I'll grant you *magic sight.*"

The serpent's mouth closed on its tail
And formed a spokeless wheel;
It disappeared in cosmic light,
Its message to reveal.
Young Squeaky called, "Don't go away!
How can I conquer fear?"
No answer came, but Squeaky saw
His grandad sitting near.

A crater centered in the light,
And it was deep and wide.
"This cosmic light," said Mother Earth,
"Will keep us unified."
Then Squeaky knew he had been taught
A lesson pure and good—
That earth was blessed with cosmic light,
The light of brotherhood.

The crater filled with molten ore—
Raw iron and pure gold,
Whose yellow blended with the red,
Its magic to unfold.
And when the red and yellow met,
All saw an orange ray.
It was so bright it made the sprites
Feel happy, warm, and gay.

Good Mother Earth now caught this ray,
And quietly she spun
An orange robe for earth god Go,
Her young and only son.
She gently called, "Come forth, my son,
And manifest yourself.
We have grave news to tell to you
From Baw, our master elf."

Then Squeaky saw the earth god Go,
A black and handsome youth.
He wore his robe of orange flame,
Protecting him in truth.
Good Mother Earth and her son, Go,
Sang praises sweet and clear;
When praises fill discouraged hearts,
There is no room for fear.

"I thank you, Mother," sang young Go,
"For this protective robe.
May you produce and share with all.
May peace rest on your globe."
The earth sprites answered with glad song,
As Grandad whispered low,
"Sing, Squeaky, praise our living soil—
Through gratitude we grow."

"Why sing so much?" asked Squeaky Voice.
Old grandad nudged his arm,
Then whispered low, "The song of praise
Produces magic charm.
I've seen young Go walk on the soil
And grieve in silent pain
When selfish men refused to share
Their overflow of grain.

"I've seen him wear that orange robe
In snow or flower dell.
He guards the gold for Mother Earth
And rules our sense of smell."
Then Squeaky lifted up his voice
And sang so very loud
That all the sprites began to grin;
Of Squeaky they were proud.

They sweetly sang, "We praise our soil
In garden and in field.
We thank you, Mother Earth and Go,
For your abundant yield."
As Squeaky finished this glad song,
He heard these words from Go,

*Then Squeaky saw the earth god Go,*
*A black and handsome youth.*
*He wore his robe of orange flame,*
*Protecting him in truth.*

"My greetings, Baw and nature sprites.
  What do you wish to know?"

Red Baw replied, "We need to know
  How we can warn King Sun—
Black Mara steals his Magic Lamp
  Before this night is done."
"One nature-night," said Go to Baw,
  "Begins right now with fall.
We sleep six months, and then awake
  When Spring sends forth her call.

"One spring and summer make six months:
  This is one nature-day.
All growing things produce their kind
  While light shows them the way.
All growing things will seek the light
  But shun all earthly strife.
King Sun sends forth his cosmic rays
  To quicken earthly life.

"These rays come from his Magic Lamp—
  Our earth requires its light.
Together we will help King Sun
  Objectify his might.
Observe what light will really do
  On arid, desert land."
When Squeaky saw fruit trees with fruit,
  He tried to understand.

The Fruit Trees sang, "We bring our fruit
  And thank you, Mother Earth,
For giving us the chance to share
  Our fruit and wholesome mirth."
"Come, let us give our fruit away,"
  Laughed Granny Apple-Tree.
"My apples make a heavy load.
  They are too much for me."

"I know where we can have some fun,"
  Said sweet, young Nellie Pear.
"Your apples make nice, round, red balls.
  Come, let us hurry there."
Then Squeaky saw an orphans' home.
  The Trees went crowding in.
"Wake up! Play ball!" called Nellie Pear.
  "We love a healthy din."

The way those children caught that fruit,
  Sun-ripened, fresh, and sweet—
The Fruit Trees stayed until each child
  Had all each child could eat.
Beneath each pillow Granny hid
  Her apples, hard and red.
"We thank you, Granny Apple-Tree,"
  The children laughed and said.

The Trees then sought an old-folks' home,
  So hurried on their way.
The old folks wakened when they heard

Sweet laughter, young and gay.
With love-shorn hearts they sat and peered
Through wise but dimming eyes;
But when they saw the Fruit Trees there,
They laughed in glad surprise.

Bananas, apples, peaches, pears
Went sailing through the air.
The old folks feasted and gave thanks
As each received a share.
"You shared our burden," laughed the Trees.
"We now feel light and free.
When one possesses too much wealth,
A fetter it can be.

"We seek the lonely ones on earth,
And those in ailing health—
This fruit is blessed by Mother Earth
From her abundant wealth."
Good Mother Earth and her son, Go,
Now whispered to Red Baw,
"Our sprites have learned their lesson well—
To share is nature's law."

*Her dark face beamed with growing smiles;*
*Her winter curls were white—*
*They jiggled with each step she took,*
*To Squeaky's great delight.*

## SQUEAKY VOICE MEETS WATER GOD APAS, NEPTUNE, UNDINE, AND SHE-WOLF

As all the Fruit Trees disappeared,
Young Go heard Squeaky say,
"When Grandad's old I'll care for him—
He can't be sent away."
Young Go replied, "One thought like that
About our lonely old
Is much more precious, Squeaky Voice,
Than all our earthly gold."

Old grandad blinked a happy tear.
His eyes were getting dim.
The elves agreed with Squeaky Voice,
For they respected him.
To earn the gift of magic sight,
One must be kind and true—
For magic sight is hidden in
The inner heart of you.

Young Go then said to Mother Earth,
Who stood in deepened thought,
"Some sprite must swim old Shadow Moat.
With danger it is fraught.
Sea water fills this darkened moat
Surrounding Mara's place,
And none but water nymphs can swim
This rough and maddened race.

"Come, Mother, call our water god:
Good Apas we must find.
We need his help. Please call him forth,
For he is good and kind.
No god can manifest in form
Upon your earthly globe
Until you make from color-tone
His own protective robe.

"Good Apas loves our planet earth
  And rules our silver ore;
Without fresh water, none can live.
  His help we must implore."
Good Mother Earth then called aloud,
  "Come, sprites, we must make haste—
Good Apas will be glad to help.
  He rules our sense of taste.

"He wonders why a thirsty child
  Will gulp a sweet drink first,
When water is the only way
  That one can quench a thirst."
Then Squeaky made the earth sprites laugh
  As he called out to say,
"School kids give me their milk to drink
  When I go there to play.

"One little girl has magic sight,
  For she can really see
Our fairy queen—and rainbows too.
  She sings her songs to me.
School kids play baseball, yell and shout,
  And make a lot of noise.
To train their sight, I hide their ball—
  But only from the boys."

"Come, come," called Go, although he laughed
  In boyish, carefree mirth.
"Come, Squeaky Voice and all you sprites,
  And help good Mother Earth."
Around the crater all the sprites
  Now circled as before.
And as they sang, the crater filled
  With seething, molten ore.

The iron gave its brilliant red;
  The silver gave its blue.
A purple mist now spiraled high,
  Its color deep and true.
As Squeaky watched this purple mist
  Arise from crater wide,
He saw it swirl into a robe
  Above the ocean tide.

In purple robe good Apas stood—
  He was quite brown and tall.
He welcomed them with outstretched hands,
  And rain began to fall.
Old grandad said, "Good Apas comes.
  He's jolly as can be—
That's why you hear the rivers laugh
  When running to the sea.

"When Apas laughs the earth-folk say,
  'Just listen to that rain.'
Dry lakes and rivers drink their fill
  From mountain, hill, and plain."
Good Apas walked above the waves,
  Then entered Silver Glade.

He called in jolly voice, "Come, come,
Why are you so afraid?

"Don't look so worried, Mother Earth.
We help each other live.
To you and man and growing things,
Fresh water I will give.

Good water comes in many forms,
As all your Seasons know.
When sleeping, you are covered by
My blankets made of snow.

"My mist and dew make fairy lakes,
Where baby nymphs can play.
Come now and hear my ocean boom,
And taste its salty spray."
"No time to waste," said Mother Earth,
But patient was her smile.
"Black Mara plots against King Sun—
Our light he would defile.

"He plans to steal the Magic Lamp,
So we have sent for you.
Some sprite must swim old Shadow Moat.
We need your counsel true."
Good Apas said, "My nymphs will help;
They keep me well informed.
They filled the rivers full last night
(But earth-folk said it stormed).

"My water nymphs just love to swim,
And dive and race and float.
My youngest grandchild, brave Undine,
Will swim old Shadow Moat."
"I run as fast," said Squeaky Voice,
"As your Undine can swim."

"You'll have to prove it," Grandad said,
  Then gently chided him.

Good Apas said, "Don't scold him, Baw.
  Your grandchild is like mine—
Although too brash, they tell the truth;
  This attribute is fine.
I must call Neptune, my fine son,
  The father of Undine.
He teaches her aquatic feats;
  She is our swimming queen.

"My ocean slumbers in its might:
  Son Neptune lies asleep.
He rules my oceans, but Undine
  Rules all my waves so deep.
Son Neptune worships wise King Sun
  But scolds his naughty Beams
Because they drink no salty drink
  But sip from lakes and streams.

"He blames these happy Sunbeams bright
  And says it is their fault—
When drawing water from his seas,
  They fill his bed with salt."
Young Squeaky laughed as Apas called,
  "Come, Neptune, show thy might!
Black Mara steals the Magic Lamp,
  Which gives the world its light."

All saw old Neptune cleave the sea
  In answer to the call;
His ocean raced through Shadow Moat
  And boomed against its wall.
Old Neptune rose through briny foam
  And shook his great, white head.
He rubbed his sleepy eyes and roared,
  "Who called me from my bed?"

"I called," said Apas to his son.
  "Come, Neptune, did you hear?"
"Aye, aye," said Neptune with a yawn.
  "I have a right good ear.
I heard about Black Mara's plan—
  That vile and evil scamp—
He waits until King Sun rides north
  To steal his Magic Lamp."

Good Apas called, "Awaken, then,
  And help protect King Sun.
His Magic Lamp gives light to all.
  Come fight the Evil One!"
Old Neptune said, "I'll call Undine—
  No water nymph can drown.
She swims and drives 'round Shadow Moat;
  Her feats are of renown."

How Squeaky and the sprites did laugh
  When Neptune called Undine—
She answered him by splashing him

*How Squeaky and the sprites did laugh*
*When Neptune called Undine—*
*She answered him by splashing him*
*With waves of silver sheen!*

With waves of silver sheen!
They watched this lovely, suntanned maid
Pat Neptune's bearded cheek;
She combed the seaweed from his hair
And gave his ear a tweak.

Old Neptune laughed and called to her,
"We have much work to do;
We watch Black Mara and his men,
So I am sending you.
We must get word to wise King Sun.
Go watch these evil knaves,
But do not swim through Shadow Moat—
Drive high upon our waves.

"Watch closely when their drawbridge drops;
Watch all who come and go.
Black Mara's power is so great
He makes an evil foe.
I'll make our ocean wild and fierce
And raise an angry tide,
That you might see above the moat
As 'round and 'round you ride."

Then Neptune filled his cheeks with air
And blew it out in gales.
From ocean foam, sea horses came
And swished their pointed tails.
Impatiently they shook their heads
But held them proud and high.
They pawed the waves to silver mist
And tossed it to the sky.

Undine called forth her seashell coach
From Neptune's ocean floor;
The horses formed in four long lines,
Just twice an even score.
Undine stepped in her pink-shell coach;
The horses hitched themselves.
The mermaids and the water nymphs
All hailed the watching elves.

Undine then held her ribbon reins
And drove with laughter gay.
The Moonbeams kissed her cheeks and hair

Through perfumed, salty spray.
Her dress was made from sea-green grass,
With trailing sash of white.
Black Mara's guards could not see her—
They had no magic sight.

Undine drove 'round old Shadow Moat,
Then slowed her prancing steeds.
She gathered ballast for her coach—
Brown kelp and ocean weeds.
The nature sprites were so engrossed
In watching this mad drive,
They did not miss young Squeaky Voice
Until they saw him dive.

For Squeaky Voice had climbed a tree
Whose branches were outspread
Above old Shadow Moat's great wall,
Where guards were heard to tread.
Young Squeaky watched until Undine
Drove right beneath his feet,
Then dropped upon her seashell coach.
His timing was quite neat.

Undine called out, "You foolish elf!
I'm glad you are alive.
You know you elves can't swim or float.
Why did you make that dive?"
"To cross the moat," said Squeaky Voice,
"And do things you can't do.
The way to Mara's house is black,
And filled with pitfalls too."

Undine replied, "Then hang on tight.
The tide is seaweed brown.
I'll push you high to inner wall—
It's safe and you won't drown."
A guard called out, "The sea is wild
And filled with seaweed kelp.
Old She-Wolf feeds her hungry pups.
I hear them howl and yelp.

"Watch sharp and shoot all moving things.
Black Mara's in a stew.
He sent his runners out again
And told them what to do."
"Did you hear that?" asked Squeaky Voice.
"It's time for me to jump."
Undine pushed Squeaky on the wall,
Upon a seaweed clump.

Her horses reared and threw the guards
In rough and raging tide
While Squeaky ran to She-Wolf's cave,
Where he could safely hide.
For he had played in there before—
Old She-Wolf was his friend.
She knew the nature sprites were kind—
On them she could depend.

*Young Squeaky watched until Undine*
*Drove right beneath his feet,*
*Then dropped upon her seashell coach.*
*His timing was quite neat.*

She scolded Squeaky; then she said,
"Be careful of my pup.
My puppies are too full to play,
And tired of being up."
"You go to sleep," said Squeaky Voice.
"I'll dry my clothes awhile."
Old She-Wolf drew her puppies close
And curled up with a smile.

Above her den, the wall caved in
And closed the cave up tight.
Old She-Wolf pushed against the rocks:
They did not budge a mite.
Young Squeaky said, "Don't push. You're safe.
Just make your puppies sleep.

I'll go for help since I can climb
Where others cannot creep.

"I first must go to Mara's den;
Then I'll come back to you.
He plans to steal the Magic Lamp
From wise King Sun so true."
"I hate Black Mara," She-Wolf growled.
"He used black-magic art
To change my human form to wolf.
He has an evil heart.

"He changed my form but not my soul.
*He* is more beast than man.
I too can help the nature gods
To thwart Black Mara's plan.
He must not steal the Magic Lamp!
Through light we learn to grow;
It blesses us if we will try
To understand and know.

"Men think all animals are beasts.
Our instinct they condemn.
But since most men have thinking minds,
We animals blame them.
No animal will kill for gold—
Existence is our strife.
Earth-men fear us and we fear them.
And each protects his life.

"Some men will hoard, through selfish greed,
Much more than they can use.
The law of nature hides the truth
In forms that men abuse."
Then She-Wolf lifted high her head
And howled with all her might
To warn her friends in darkened wood
To guard their instinct-light.

Some animals heard She-Wolf call,
And they arose from sleep
And went to guard the Silver Glade,
Their nature tryst to keep.
Young Squeaky grinned when next he heard
These wolves begin to howl—
Black Mara's men would stay indoors
When wolves were on the prowl.

## SQUEAKY VOICE MEETS GOLDEN FAY, AIR GOD VAYU, AND HOOT OWL

Young Squeaky heard the howling wolves
Beyond old She-Wolf's cave.
"Do you fear Mara?" Squeaky asked.
"You seem so strong and brave."
Old She-Wolf growled, "Not for myself,
But for my children here.
Black magic is an evil thing.
Its power lies in fear.

"Fight fear, my lad, with all your heart.
It is a dreadful foe.
Black Mara fears the light of truth,
As all of us well know.
Before he changed me to a wolf,
I was a princess fair.
I would not worship his black art,
Which makes good men despair."

"We elves hate evil," Squeaky said.
"Black Mara's heart is vile.
My grandad says he tricks earth-men
Through selfish greed and guile."
"Your grandad knows," old She-Wolf said
With fierce and angry growl.
"Black Mara changes men to beasts
And turns them loose to prowl.

"I fear all men who have no souls—
They are Black Mara's beasts.
I hear these men and watch them dine
At their nocturnal feasts."
Again old She-Wolf bared her fangs
And howled her ageless hate
Of those who use the innocent
As pawns of lustful fate.

Black Mara's men heard She-Wolf howl,
And terror filled each heart;
Full well they knew beast instinct was
Their own vile counterpart.
"Stop howling, She-Wolf," Squeaky said.
"Your puppies are afraid."
Old She-Wolf growled, "I must dig out.
Too long have I delayed.

"I have in here the thing I need
To free me from this cave,
And it will help me while I dig—
My puppies I must save."
Young Squeaky said, "You're trapped in here.
I see no one but me,
And I'm too small to lift these rocks.
Whatever can it be?"

Old She-Wolf answered as she dug,
"We have fresh air in here.
If we give thanks for this fresh air,
An air sylph will appear.
Although my good self is unknown,
I'm grateful for this air—
Do men give thanks for nature's gifts
That bless them everywhere?"

"All children do," said Squeaky Voice.
"They're grateful when they say,
'The air is sweet; the rain is good.'
I hear them when we play."
Old She-Wolf lifted up her nose
And sang her praises high;
Then Squeaky heard right in the cave
A tiny voice reply.

"I heard you praise our living air.
My name is Golden Fay.
Each plane has helpers who will come
And guide you on your way.
A sylph has carried on the air
Your message to your mate;
He tunnels now to set you free.
You have not long to wait.

"Our air god Vayu sent me here.
He rules our magic sight.
Your being grateful for the air
Showed him you served the light."
Old She-Wolf said, "I do thank you
For bringing help to me.
All animals obey King Sun,
Whose light will set us free.

"I hear my mate—how fast he digs!
We soon will be outside,
Beyond Black Mara's evil law,
Whose power I defied."
As She-Wolf greeted her wolf-mate,
Their pups began to yelp.

Each wolf then carried from the cave
  A fat, contented whelp.

The wolves then disappeared in light.
  Their battle had been won.
Said Golden Fay, "Come, Squeaky Voice,
  And let us have some fun.
Come, let us race as I return
  To Vayu, kind and wise.

For he must know Black Mara's plan
  And how you heard his spies.

"We sylphs fly faster than you run;
  In nature all must share;
Fast flying is the work we do
  To purify the air.
We sylphs enjoy our work and play,
  And travel very far.

Some children see our crowns of light
And think each crown a star.

"How do you like my wings of jade?
I fold them when at rest.
All sylphs can fly or talk or sing,
To entertain a guest."
"Girls talk too much," teased Squeaky Voice.
"We boys are taught to think."
When Golden Fay began to laugh,
He blushed a rosy pink.

"My brothers race," said Golden Fay,
"Around this hemisphere.
They fly two thousand miles an hour
To clear our atmosphere."
"I'll win this race," laughed Squeaky Voice.
"How fast can girl-sylphs fly?"

"I'll show you now," said Golden Fay
As swiftly she flew by.

When Squeaky saw how fast she flew,
He called with boyish grin,
"You sylphs can fly too fast for me;
I know I cannot win."
"Keep still and watch," said Golden Fay;
Then Squeaky saw appear
A silver light of swirling air
That shimmered bright and clear.

Around this light the air sylphs flew
And waved their tiny hands.
They fanned the air across the seas
And over silent lands.
The air was filled with jeweled stars
That sparkled clear and bright.
Then Golden Fay began to chant
Within this silver light.

"Wise Vayu, this is Squeaky Voice—
The grandson of Red Baw,
Who teaches elves that life is one,
The truth in nature's law.
Come, Squeaky Voice," said Golden Fay.
"Your time has come to speak.
Wise Vayu knows, through magic sight,
True light is what you seek."

"I see no god," said Squeaky Voice.
"I fear things I can't see.
If your god Vayu is so wise,
Ask him to speak to me."
But Squeaky wished inside his heart
For Grandad, wise and true—
He wished he had not run away.
What should he say or do?

A quiet voice now spoke to him,
"Fear not the god of air.
Your wish is for your grandad elf,
So I will send you there.
Old Shadow Moat surrounds you, lad.
You must get out of here.
My Golden Fay will pilot you
Across this moat of fear."

"Come, Squeaky Voice," said Golden Fay.
"You will return on wings;
I have an airplane safe and true.
It talks, but never sings."
The air sylphs laughed at Squeaky Voice
And seized him by his coat;
They dropped him on a feathered plane
That flew across the moat.

"This plane is warm," said Squeaky Voice,
Then heard with troubled frown,
"I would not wonder," from the plane

As it went flying down.
"Hello," said Grandad to the plane.
"What brings you here, old owl?
Your yellow eyes gleam fierce and bright
Beneath your feathered cowl."

"Wise Vayu sent me," said the owl,
"And with his best regards.
You'd better spank your Squeaky Voice—
Our progress he retards."
Then Squeaky felt himself plumped off
In front of Grandad Elf.
"Where have you been?" old grandad asked.
"Come, lad, explain yourself."

But Squeaky could not talk at all,
So great was his surprise;
He saw his airplane was an owl
With angry, staring eyes.
Young Squeaky Voice thought he had seen
This plane—so warm and nice—
Fly forth to dine at close of day
On frogs or snakes or mice.

Old Hoot Owl glared at Squeaky Voice,
Who quavered as he said,
"I thank you for my airplane ride—
You make a nice, warm bed.
I bet no man can make a plane
That flies as straight as you-oo-o."

"I should say not," old Hoot Owl screeched.
"If so, just tell me who-oo-o."

Then Hoot Owl flew a spiral line
And disappeared from sight.
The air sylphs laughed because they knew
Who held his wings in flight.
The nature sprites in Silver Glade
Began to laugh and shout,
Had Squeaky and the owl enjoyed
Their airplane flying bout?

Young Go then spoke, "Our time has come
To call wise Vayu here.
Come, Mother, create Vayu's robe.
He wishes to appear."
"Come form a circle, all you sprites,"
Called gentle Mother Earth.
"Sweet Spring greets Vayu with a gift—
The flower of his birth."

Around the crater all the sprites
Began to dance and sing;
Then Squeaky saw good Mother Earth
Breathe out the breath of spring.
She said as she bedecked herself
With Chinese lilies rare,
"We welcome all the yellow race
Through Vayu, god of air.

ETHEL Gesner

*But Squeaky could not talk at all,*
*So great was his surprise;*
*He saw his airplane was an owl*
*With angry, staring eyes.*

"Our gods must wear protective robes
To walk upon my sphere;
Through cosmic rays and color tones,
Our nature gods appear."
Then Mother Earth called to the stars,
"Breathe down your sapphire blue;
Transmute my lead, which Vayu rules,
To yellow gold so true."

The Mountains tossed their snow-capped heads
And said to her, quite bold,
"It seems that you depend on us
To furnish you with gold."
"Such selfishness!" said Mother Earth.
"Our ruler is King Sun.
To save his Magic Lamp of light,
A battle must be won.

"Why hoard gold as do foolish men?
Their gold returns to me.
The only thing that blesses gold
Is sharing it, you see."
The Mountains wept—they were ashamed.
Their tears made rivers flow.
The rivers purified their gold
For Mother Earth and Go.

Young Squeaky laughed when next he saw
The Baby Rivers rise;
They pushed their snow white covers off
And rubbed their sleepy eyes.
They called aloud to Mother Earth
And tossed approving heads,
"We'll fill your crater full of gold.
Accept our nugget beds.

"We do not need a golden bed—
Sweet Spring can make us run.
We would prefer a bed of rock
If we could help King Sun."
These youngsters took their nugget beds
And filled the crater wide.
Their parent mountains were ashamed,
All gone their hoarding pride.

The Sapphire Stars began to sing,
"We gladly give our blue
To wed the yellow of your gold,
To blend bright green for you."
The magic crater spun its gold;
Bright yellow did arise.
The yellow and the blue made green
To bless the stellar skies.

And when the crater disappeared,
Wise Vayu could be seen.
This bearded air-god smiled on them.
His robe was brilliant green.
He pointed upward toward the sky.
Again young Squeaky saw

The gods of nature manifest
   The magic of their law.

The Sapphire Stars had formed a crown
   Around good Mother Earth.
For eons they had rayed their joy
   When babies greeted birth.
When Sapphire Stars breathe gently down
   Through flower-perfumed night,
Somewhere on earth a child is born
   To bring you cosmic light.

Sweet star-companions come each day
   To play a little while;
Your baby laughs and welcomes them
   With happy, knowing smile.
These Sapphire Stars reflect themselves
   In every baby's eyes.
Your baby smiles and watches them
   With happy, cooing sighs.

For they remember when they too
   Were tiny stars above.
They heard your call and answered you
   To bring you cosmic love.
Some baby souls return to God
   While memory is sweet.
They smile on you from Sapphire Stars,
   Caressing you in sleep.

All babes of childless parents sleep
   In chosen, soundless rest.
The cosmic mother nurtures them
   Within her loving breast.
She cares for them and guards them well.
   And when their birth is due,
These Sapphire Stars will gently breathe
   Your baby down to you.

Wise Vayu smiled at Mother Earth
   And lifted his right hand.
Spring flowers bloomed and grass grew green
   Upon her wakened land.
The elves unrolled their shoes for bed
   And grinned in elfin pride;
They thought about young Squeaky Voice
   And Hoot Owl's airplane ride.

## SQUEAKY VOICE SEES THE EARTH'S CREATION; FIRE GOD AGNI APPEARS

Young Squeaky Voice sat up and yawned,
  Then jumped upon his feet.
Golden Fay watched as he awoke
  From his refreshing sleep.
As Squeaky grinned, she whispered low,
  "Did you enjoy your ride?
Old Hoot Owl flew you safe and true
  Above old Neptune's tide.

"Through intuition, Vayu knew
  You wished for Grandad Elf.
Your intuition is the voice
  That speaks within yourself."
"My conscience tells me," Squeaky said,
  "Exactly what to do;
But when I disobey, I know
  That nothing turns out true."

"Obey your first impression, lad,"
  Responded Golden Fay.
"It is your conscience telling you
  And showing you the way."
"School kids say 'hunches,' " Squeaky said.
  "I hear them when they call,
'I have a hunch that elf is here—
  I cannot find my ball.'

"The school kids laugh and hunt for me,
  And each obeys his hunch.
And when they find me, they can see
  I'm nibbling on their lunch."
"Earth children know," laughed Golden Fay.
  "Their hunches they can feel.
Your conscience, hunch, or inner voice
  Is true—and very real."

Wise Vayu silenced all the sprites
  By lifting his right hand.
Good Mother Earth smiled on young Go—
  Sweet Spring had blessed their land.
Wise Vayu said, "I have a plan,
  But it depends on fog.
It keeps Black Mara's men indoors—
  They fear the poison bog.

"Good Apas, make dense water fog.
  My air sylphs love to work.
When they fly in Black Mara's room,
  They will not dare to shirk.
If air sylphs do not fan the air,
  It soon becomes impure—
Black Mara's men will seek fresh air,
  Of that you may be sure.

"And when my grandchild flies inside,
  She will report to me.
Through intuition she can hear
  And taste and smell and see."
Young Squeaky said, "Another girl!
  Why don't they send a boy?"
The nature gods and Grandad laughed.
  Such candor they enjoy.

Young Squeaky blushed and hung his head
  When he heard Vayu say,
"Come, sprites, and meet my grandchild here.
  Her name is Golden Fay."
"Our Golden Fay!" gasped Squeaky Voice.
  "Granddaughter of a god?"
"She is a friend," old grandad said
  With stern and knowing nod.

"True friends will know you from their hearts
  Regardless of your name.

They love you for your own true worth
   And not for worldly fame."
"I'm sorry, Grandad," Squeaky said.
   "I spoke before I thought."
Wise Vayu said, "Old Baw speaks well.
   A lesson has been taught."

Black fog now rose from Shadow Moat,
   As dense as it could be.
The nature gods heard Mara rage—
   King Sun he could not see.
Black Mara called his council knaves
   And roared with evil leer,
"Up to our secret tower room,
   Where none can spy or hear."

The men obeyed, and each sat down.
   This room was closed up tight.
They thought themselves quite safe up here
   To plot against the light.
"If I can't get that Magic Lamp,"
   Said Mara with a curse,
"I'll blind the hearts and souls of men
   And rule this universe."

As Mara raved, old One Eye sighed,
   Then slumped upon his chair.
"Go open windows," Mara gasped.
   "We need some fresher air."
The men could hardly get their breath;
   Their heads began to spin.
One man then pushed a window up,
   And Golden Fay flew in.

Her helper sylphs then fanned the air
   And watched the men revive.
Without fresh air no breathing soul

Could very long survive.
Black Mara called, "Come, come, One Eye.
I've seen King Sun's fine home.
But no man's seen the Magic Lamp
Within the crystal dome.

"I know it burns a special oil.
But you must find a way
To make an oil to simulate
The light of King Sun's day."
Old One Eye said, "I hear strange things
About his magic oil.
His cosmic oil comes not from man,
Earth science, or the soil."

Black Mara snarled, "You ought to know—
In science you excel.
I wonder if you know some facts
That you refuse to tell.
The power of that Magic Lamp
Reflects itself in thought.
As long as children see and think,
My plans will come to naught.

"When men love power for themselves,
They sell their souls to me;
But those who worship truth and light
Help other men to see."
Golden Fay understood at last
Black Mara's evil might;
He knew when men were filled with hate,
There was no room for light.

Black Mara raged, "Come, come, One Eye.
My power don't deny
Unless you want to lose the sight
Of your remaining eye."
Old One Eye cringed from Mara's rage,
Then bravely answered him,
"You cannot blind my inner sight—
That sight is never dim.

"You blinded me, when I was young,
Through my inquiring mind.
You said I could create great things
To benefit mankind.
Your father, Mars, and wise King Sun
Knew what they were about—
When you desired to rule as God,
Your evil cast you out."

"What talk is this?" Black Mara roared
And clenched his mighty fist.
"Go to your lab and study oil.
My power don't resist."
As One Eye left the tower room,
He muttered very low,
"You bought my mind, but not my soul.
But this you do not know.

"In making things for men to use,
The maker should discern
If they be good or bad for men,
A lesson hard to learn."
Black Mara watched old One Eye go
And thought with face quite grim,
"Old One Eye needs a fine new lab
To keep my hold on him."

Black Mara then dismissed his men.
In silence they obeyed.
And Golden Fay, through heavy fog,
Flew back to Silver Glade.
Clear vision rested in this glade,
For those who sought the light.
There nature gods objectified
The power of their might.

Soon Golden Fay had told her news
And disappeared from view.
The nature gods called Mother Earth
To plan what next to do.
"Call Agni, god of fire," she said.
"He is our highest one.
With lightning he will write for us
Our message to King Sun.

"Four seasons make one day and night.
Young Go brought us the fall;
Good Apas brought the winter's rain;
Sweet Spring heard Vayu call.
Our summer comes, and Agni reigns
And purifies by fire
The hearts of those who seek the truth—
If this be their desire."

"We all seek truth," thought Squeaky Voice.
"I wonder what she meant."
And then he heard that humming tone
And started his ascent.
Among the planets he soon stood
And saw the earth so dark,
Deep nestled in its soundless sleep,
The golden sun its arc.

As Squeaky watched he now could see
The sun as it arose.
It had two long and gleaming eyes
And black, dilated nose.
Then higher, higher rose the sun
Until its mouth appeared
And opened wide and spewed out fire.
Again young Squeaky feared.

The fire then formed a lion. And
As Squeaky saw his face,
The lion challenged with a roar
The boundless solar space.
He set on fire with tongue of flame
The newborn planet earth.

He watched it burn and purify
The dross of solar birth.

The lion closed his mouth of fire;
He closed his flaming eyes.
The chastened earth began to cool
With mighty, heaving sighs.
Each sigh made mountains rise or fall,
A valley or a hill.
As eons passed a mist arose,
And then the earth grew still.

This newborn planet was baptized
With gentle, healing rain,
Which christened it as Mother Earth
And healed her travail pain.
Great water pools began to form
In canyons dark and deep;
This water wed the soil of Earth,
Arousing her from sleep.

The lion opened wide his eyes.
And then, without a sound
He touched the earth with his right paw,
And *life* flowed in the ground.
The wedded water and the soil
Gave birth to flowers rare.
Green grass and trees grew on the earth
To purify the air.

The lion struck with his left paw
The sea and desert sand;
Great monsters slithered from the sea
To lay their eggs on land.
Each egg hatched out a tiny form
That slept and moved and grew;
Some forms arose on mammal wings
And to the mountains flew.

The lion blew his breath 'round earth,
And primal wind was born—
It cleared the mist from Mother Earth,
And she beheld the morn.
This spirit-wind then upward blew
Earth flowers to the sky;
The flowers changed to singing birds
(The wind taught them to fly).

Then Squeaky saw the lion turn
And lie upon his back
To balance on his mighty paws
The planet earth so black.
His paws revolved the planet earth
And rocked it to-and-fro;
Then day brought work and night brought sleep,
To help earth children grow.

The lion's paws tipped planet earth
From south to frozen north;

It took one year for Mother Earth
  To bring her seasons forth.
In rhythmic motion Mother Earth
  Turned slowly in her place.
The lion then became a star
  Within our cosmic space.

With mighty sickle he guards earth—
  A sickle made of stars—
Protecting children who might fear
  Black Mara, son of Mars.
Young Squeaky stood in deepest thought,
  For once again he heard

That magic, humming, nature tone—
It hid the primal word.

He felt himself slowly descend
To lovely Silver Glade.
Old grandad patted Squeaky Voice,
Who now was not afraid.
The sprites then danced 'round Mother Earth.
Their singing filled the air.
The great star-lion beamed on them—
True gratitude is prayer.

Wise Vayu, Apas, and young Go
Were chanting as before.
And once again the crater filled
With seething molten ore.
Said Mother Earth to all who sang,
"We call our god of fire;
Good Agni comes to help us thwart
Black Mara's false desire."

The iron ore released its flame,
Its spirit swirling high.
Then Squeaky saw a bright red robe
Against the dawning sky.
"Come forth, god Agni," called young Go.
"Objectify thy might.
Black Mara steals our Magic Lamp,
Which gives the world its light."

Fierce lightning flashed across the sky.
All heard the lion roar.
The air sylphs flew around the earth
And rattled every door.
The people shivered in their fright;
All feared this thunderstorm.
But many saw above the clouds
A light begin to form.

The lightning ceased, and there appeared
A mighty nature-god.
In flaming robe of brilliant red,
Across the sky he trod.
Then Squeaky heard the white god speak—
Stern Agni strong and tall—
"Our Magic Lamp burns not for one
But gives its light to all.

"I go to meet our wise King Sun,
Wherever he may be.
In lightning I will write to him
Where Mara cannot see."
Through deepened silence Grandad said,
"When Agni does return,
Black Mara will be dealt a blow—
His time has come to learn."

## SQUEAKY VOICE SEES THE WISHING TREE AND MEETS A SEA GULL

The nature gods and Mother Earth
  Now scanned the dawning sky,
Expecting Agni to return
  With wise King Sun's reply.
"Come, Squeaky Voice," old grandad said.
  "Come rest awhile with me.
We'll sit beneath this evergreen.
  It is a Wishing Tree."

To Squeaky Voice this tree was new,
  So green, and so alive.
Without the wishes of a child,
  This tree could not survive.
Old grandad said to Squeaky Voice,
  "Take off your shoes and rest.
Inside your shoe-house, you will sleep—
  Our magic shoes are blessed."

Then Squeaky heard that humming tone,
  Which sailed him into space.
The Wishing Tree began to laugh
  At Squeaky's sober face.
He stood inside an orphans' home,
  Its sick ward filled with beds
Where crippled children and the ill
  Turned restless, sleeping heads.

Pine fragrance wafted through the ward;
  Then Squeaky saw appear
A light—dissolving doors and walls,
  So all could see and hear.
The Wishing Tree began to sing.
  The children all awoke.
Some rubbed their eyes; some laughed aloud,
  Believing it a joke.

Each child could see the Wishing Tree
   And hear it singing there.
Its gifts were made from wishes true.
   What joy it was to share!
"Come, make your wishes," laughed the Tree.
   The children looked around.
Each made a wish, and then *all* heard
   That magic, singing sound.

New toys now landed on each bed
   In answer to each wish.
Then Squeaky heard an airplane zoom
   And heard a rustling swish.
This swishing noise, you may have guessed,
   Was made by dollies gay—
They wore their best brocades and silks
   To come in there and play.

Oh, how they swished their lovely gowns
   As gaily they did dance!
Then suddenly they stopped, amazed,
   And stood as in a trance.
Young Squeaky laughed as he next saw
   Toy soldiers dressed in red.
"We're tired of playing war," they laughed.
   "Please dance with us instead."

"Go back and entertain the boys,"
   One dolly said, quite pert.
"Those ailing boys have wished for you—
   Their feelings will be hurt."
The soldiers bowed. The dollies blushed;
   The pert one tossed her curls.
Each soldier chose a lovely doll
   And danced in spinning whirls.

And as the children watched them dance,
   They felt their beds arise.
As if on airplanes, they now sailed
   Through magic, stellar skies.
The airplanes flew them 'round the world.
   The children laughed in fun.

And when the airplanes brought them back,
Each crippled child could run.

The mute could talk. The deaf could hear.
The blind could plainly see.
Oh, how they laughed and danced with joy
Around the Wishing Tree!
At last the orphan children slept
In magic, healing light.
The cosmic mother disappeared
In silent, purple night.

Old grandad wakened Squeaky Voice,
Who rose with grinning yawn.
They bowed their heads in gratitude
To greet the coming dawn.
Old grandad said, "The dawn grows bright—
Stern Agni must be nigh—
His robe of red reflects itself
Against our morning sky."

When Agni strode in Silver Glade,
The gods surrounded him.
And as they listened to his news,
They all grew very grim.
Wise Vayu said to Squeaky Voice,
"Come, go with Golden Fay.
Seek One Eye in Black Mara's lab,
But go your secret way.

"Tell One Eye that you bring to him
This message from King Sun:
'Please bring your oil to Silver Glade
And show what you have done.
To prove the power of the truth—
Black magic versus white—
We challenge you. And as you know,
Black Mara, we will fight!

" 'King Sun protects his Magic Lamp.
Its oil burns clear and true.
It gives its light to all earth-men
And not a chosen few.' "
Young Squeaky Voice and Golden Fay
Kept quiet as they heard
Their nature gods begin to chant
That singing, humming word.

The air sylphs and the water nymphs
Were ready to obey;
They watched fire genies blink their eyes
And earth sprites in their play.
"I'll have to cross the moat again,"
Young Squeaky said to Go.
"I'm glad old Hoot Owl is asleep—
His flying is too slow.

"Young Scatter Wind flies very fast—
He whizzes through the air.
I watch men-pilots dive their planes—

They fly most everywhere."
Wise Vayu smiled and said to Go,
"Your Squeaky wants a thrill.
Let Apas call a water fowl
To test young Squeaky's skill."

Good Apas called, "Come, Squeaky Voice.
A sea gull you may ride.
And he is stupid as a plane,
So you must be his guide.
This seaweed makes a nice, tight rein
To hold his head up high—
For he must see no ocean waves
If you intend to fly.

"For if he is a hungry gull
And sees a swimming fish,
Then he will dive and wet you, lad,
To get his breakfast dish."
"I'll hold his head," laughed Squeaky Voice,
"So high he cannot see
His breakfast dish of swimming fish.
Your gull will not dunk me."

But Squeaky spoke a mite too soon—
The gull had hungry eyes.
He saw a fish and dived for it,
To Squeaky's great surprise.
The sea gull missed his breakfast dish,
Then downward dropped his head.
Young Squeaky tried to make him fly;
The sea gull dived instead.

He tried to throw young Squeaky off—
He dived and zoomed and croaked.
But Squeaky held the reins so tight
The sea gull nearly choked.
At last the sea gull caught a shrimp,
Then headed for the shore;
He gulped it down, then looked around—
The sea gull wanted more.

He landed on Black Mara's beach
And plumped wet Squeaky down.
The water nymphs and mermaids laughed
At Squeaky's thoughtful frown.
Called Golden Fay, "Run fast, and dry,
Because you are quite wet.
If you keep active, you will find
You have no time to fret.

"Is that the way you take your bath?
It must be lots of fun.
I know you had a thrilling ride,
But now it's time to run."
Young Squeaky raced towards Mara's place
With laughing Golden Fay.
A salamander called to them,
"I know the safest way."

He took them through a tunnel deep;
And in its farthest end,
Old One Eye stood with testing tube—
His true and closest friend.
"We bring a message from King Sun,"
Said Squeaky, running in.
As One Eye listened to the news,
He rubbed his bearded chin.

"I hate what Mara did to me,"
Old One Eye slowly said.
"You children hide; I'll call him here.
He just went up to bed."
When Mara heard the news, he roared,
"Who told King Sun our plan?
When I find out, I'll strike him down—
Be he a god or man.

"The nature gods use Silver Glade
As their nocturnal camp.
It will give me a chance to steal
King Sun's true Magic Lamp.
My magic is as great as his—
Of him I'm not afraid.
Prepare your oil to meet King Sun
Tonight in Silver Glade.

"The power of that Magic Lamp
Lies hidden in its oil."
Then Mara stamped back to his room
To gloat upon his spoil.
Young Squeaky Voice and Golden Fay
Went quietly outside,
And then they raced to Shadow Moat
To cross its ebbing tide.

They met the sea gull, which complained
With hoarse, discordant cry,
"I am so full of juicy shrimp
I do not care to fly.
I'll hop the waves to take you back.
I do not dare to see
A swimming fish or juicy shrimp—
It may look good to me."

"Don't dive again," said Squeaky Voice.
"You are a greedy gull.
No glutton has a thinking mind.
No wonder you are dull."
The gull flew low with Squeaky Voice.
His landing was quite neat.
The sprites then raced toward Silver Glade,
Their journey to complete.

When Agni heard their news, he said,
"I'll go to meet King Sun.
Black Mara's cycle closes soon.
His test has now begun."
The nature gods dismissed their groups.
Each group sought needed rest.

*He tried to throw young Squeaky off—*
*He dived and zoomed and croaked.*
*But Squeaky held the reins so tight*
*The sea gull nearly choked.*

"We meet tonight," said Mother Earth,
"To watch Black Mara's test."

"Why go to sleep?" asked Squeaky Voice,
Excited as could be.
"Could Mara hurt us while we sleep?
His test I want to see."
"We sleep till midnight," Grandad said.
"Please rest—be not afraid—
The fire of Agni will protect
All sprites in Silver Glade.

"Unroll your shoes and go to bed.
I do not want to scold.
If you deny your heart its dreams,
Your body will grow old."
"Be sure and wake me," Squeaky said,
But hearing no reply,
He settled down and went to sleep,
Relaxing with a sigh.

Deep silence reigned in Silver Glade—
All nature sprites now slept.

They did not hear the prowling beasts
As through the woods they crept.
The beasts had heard old She-Wolf call,
And those that understood
Now listened as she talked to them
Beyond Black Mara's wood.

They did not know that she had been
A maiden young and fair;
For eons she had guided them
Away from beastly lair.
Old She-Wolf said, "You must not kill
But only to exist;
Survival-of-the-fittest law
Is one we must resist."

Some wolves resented this and growled,
Their eyes like balls of fire.
"Let instinct guide you," She-Wolf said,
"And not your beast desire."
Then She-Wolf saw in Agni's fire
A genie of the flame,
Who said to her, "I come to change
Your beastly form and name.

"When Mara met you as a maid,
He tried to buy your youth,
So he could use you to deceive
Your friends of light and truth.
Because you would not sell your soul,
He changed your form through hate.
But you still sought the light and truth,
Redeeming beast estate.

"Surround the Silver Glade tonight
And watch Black Mara's test.
Be not afraid but watch the light—
The truth will manifest.
If Mara wins, you will remain
A wolf, despised by man.
But you will have another chance—
One life is just a span.

"If wise King Sun can win this test
And make Black Mara see
The light within the human soul,
A maiden you will be."
The genie changed to flaming torch
Of swirling, golden light.
It centered in the Silver Glade
To guard throughout the night.

Some animals that feared the flame
Crept back where it was dark.
"Guard instinct," She-Wolf called to them,
"If it be just a spark.
Our instinct-light will set us free
And help us to evolve.
If I become a maid again,
Your fear I will absolve."

Some animals agreed with her—
These were the ones she chose
To guard the Silver Glade of light.
She felt her wolf-days close.
She wondered, as she faced the glade
And saw the torch of flame,
If Mara would behold it too
As through the woods he came.

She had no terror in her heart,
For she had always known
That animal and sprite and man
Must reap what each has sown.
Would she remain a hated wolf
Or be a lovely maid?
She put her head upon her paws
And faced the Silver Glade.

## THE NATURE GODS TEST BLACK MARA

"Awaken, Squeaky," Grandad said.
  "The hour approaches one.
Black Mara rides toward Silver Glade;
  His soul test has begun."
"Awaken, sprites," called Mother Earth,
  Insisting, with her plea,
"We must encircle Silver Glade,
  Black Mara's test to see."

Good Mother Earth began to chant
  A prayer sweet and low;
Then Squeaky saw the flaming torch
  Arise in golden glow.
This golden glow began to swirl
  Against the darkened night,
And there it formed a golden cross,
  A chalice for the light.

Then into Silver Glade there rode
  Black Mara and his men.
For safety they each wore chain mail,
  Their bodies to defend.
In arrogance they sat their mounts,
  With trappings of gold braid.
Through lifted visors they beheld
  A darkened Silver Glade.

Then through the darkness, Mara's eyes
  Beheld the cross of gold.
But nothing else in Silver Glade
  Could Mara's eyes behold.
Old grandad nudged young Squeaky Voice,
  Then whispered in his ear,
"Watch Mara's evil, cunning tricks
  To conquer men through fear.

"Watch Mara. He can see no light—
To him it has no worth.
But he has seen the cross of gold,
Man's test on planet earth."
Then Squeaky heard Black Mara call,
"Your wise King Sun I seek.
He bade me come and bring my oil.
With him I wish to speak."

Black Mara startled when he heard,
"Prepare yourself to learn

How cosmic law protects the light,
Which you defile and spurn.
For eons you have preyed on men—
You are the Evil One.
You come to steal from planet earth
The light of wise King Sun.

"I warn you that the nature gods
Were told your evil plan.
These gods protect the Magic Lamp
That gives its light to man."
"I fear no gods," Black Mara roared.
"That lamp I came to see.
Come show yourself or bring King Sun,
Wherever he may be."

Deep silence reigned in Silver Glade.
All wings now ceased to fly.
A stillness settled on the earth,
The ocean, air, and sky.
This heavy silence soon became
Unbearable suspense;
While Mara fumed in angry thought,
His waiting men grew tense.

"It's dark enough to steal that cross,"
Was Mara's evil thought.
"My magic would protect me, too—
I've never yet been caught."
As his vile thought went forth in space,
All heard the thunder crash
And saw a fireball in the sky
Send forth a flaming flash.

"That fireball," whispered Grandad Elf,
"Seeks our magnetic land.
Remember, lad, to conquer fear
The heart must understand.
Your lesson lies within the light,
Not in the cross of gold.
This cosmic light is part of you
And helps your soul unfold."

The fireball dropped around the cross,
For this was holy ground.
And from the flaming fire there came
That magic, humming sound.
The fire flamed upward 'round the cross,
Protecting cosmic light
From those who worshiped gold instead
Of magic pure and white.

As Mara and his men drew back,
Their horses squealed and reared;
Their instincts warned them that a fire
Was something to be feared.
Then suddenly these horses stood,
As quiet as could be.
Old One Eye called, "What causes this?
Cannot our horses see?"

But One Eye knew within his heart
  Their horses were not blind
But were protected by the light,
  Which could not be confined.
As Mara sat in wicked thought,
  Old One Eye called his name.
"Look up above the cross of gold—
  A god protects its flame."

Black Mara looked above the cross,
  Then nodded angry head;
He saw the great, white god of fire,
  In robe of brilliant red.
"That god is Agni," One Eye called.
  "He rules our magic North.
No wonder fire protects the cross—
  His power brought it forth."

All saw stern Agni lift his hand;
  Then with bright red he drew
A circle 'round the Silver Glade,
  Of magic pure and true.
This circle changed to roaring fire,
  Of fierce and flaming might.
Black Mara cursed beneath his breath
  As he beheld his plight.

His frightened men called out to him
  In jeering, vile disdain,
"Where has your magic power gone—
  Or did you boast in vain?
Can you not challenge nature gods
  As well as wise King Sun?"
Old One Eye called, "Put out the fire
  And prove how it is done."

Black Mara knew he must restore
  Old One Eye's faith in him.
He called black-magic words, and lo!

The fire began to dim.
All watching eyes in Silver Glade
Could see the fire abate.
"Come, let us go," old One Eye called,
"Before it is too late."

The fire burned down, and Squeaky said
While plucking Grandad's sleeve,
"How can Black Mara dim the fire?
What gods does he believe?"
Old grandad said, "Black-magic gods
Can dim your outer eyes;
Just watch Black Mara and his men
And witness their surprise.

"The way one uses power, lad,
Makes magic black or white.
Black magic blinds the truth in man;
White magic brings him light."
Old One Eye called, "The fire abates—
Come, Mara, let us go."
Their horses would not move but neighed,
Their greetings to bestow.

Old One Eye cried, "The water god!
I now can comprehend
The reason why our horses neigh—
They recognize a friend."
All eyes beheld in purple robe
Good Apas take his stand.

The west side of the cross was his
To guard the sea and land.

He drew his circle far beyond
The fire and Silver Glade.
(Old One Eye jeered at Mara's men—
He saw they were afraid.)
This circle changed to open sea,
Its water rough and wide.
Around stern Agni's burning fire,
It rushed with mighty tide.

"I must placate these nature gods,"
Was Mara's cunning thought.
"Too bad they worship truth and light—
Such gods cannot be bought.
I must find out how strong they are
Before I dare assail;
But when I find their weakest point,
My magic will prevail."

With flattery Black Mara called,
"Your magic I admire.
To do as well as you have done,
I would not dare aspire.
You nature gods must surely know
King Sun sent word to me
To bring my oil and meet him here.
Good sirs, where can he be?"

No answer came, but from the East
All saw a green-robed god
Upon the ether wave of light.
He came with knowing nod.
"Wise Vayu," One Eye firmly said,
"The mighty god of air.
Come, Mara, you must welcome him—
His wisdom you might share."

Wise Vayu stood beside the cross—
The East was his by right.
All saw the yellow god of air
Objectify his might.
Beyond the fire and raging sea,
He drew his circle true.
Old One Eye knew these nature gods
Had planned what each would do.

All saw wise Vayu's circle form
A mighty, surging wall
Of shrieking, screaming, demon wind,
Which screeched with fiendish call.
Then faster, faster raced the wind
Around the raging sea.
The folks of earth could hear it wail
From mountain to the lea.

Some said, "Ghost demons ride tonight.
We hear their piercing screams."
The knowing ones kept silent tongues,
Dismissing it as dreams.
Young Squeaky Voice took Grandad's hand
And held it in his own.
"That wind is terrible," he said.
"Why does it cry and moan?"

"It is the wall of wailing souls,"
Then whispered Grandad Elf.
"They are the ghosts of evil men
Who worshiped greed and self.
Black Mara fears our nature gods,
Although he seems so bold.
He knows these souls belong to him,
For he bought them with gold.

"These screams have frightened Mara's men.
Unguarded are their eyes.
When truth disturbs an evil man,
Its power he denies."
Old One Eye called, "Come, Mara. Come
Make good your bragging boasts,
Or you might join your screaming friends—
Those fiendish, evil ghosts."

Black Mara cursed and spurred his horse;
It vaulted him up high.
He disappeared from Silver Glade,
Up through the darkened sky.
His flight was stopped as he now felt
A firm, restraining hand—

It righted him and seated him
   In darkened, foreign land.

As Mara vanished Squeaky heard
   That singing, humming tone;
Then once again he stood in space,
   But he was not alone.
Young Squeaky saw a dragon form
   Into a living chair,
And right beneath its crested head,
   Was Mara sitting there.

While Mara gazed in darkened space,
   A voice to him did speak,
"You come to steal our Magic Lamp.
   No wisdom do you seek.
You have no power in this realm,
   Which you will soon discern.
Before you use our Magic Lamp,
   Its secret you must learn.

"We worship here a god of light,
   So we will grant to you

The right to prove your self-made god
And show what he can do."
"My god has power," Mara jeered,
Then shook his mighty fist.
"Most men will worship wealth and gold—
A god that few resist."

The voice replied, "Some men have wealth
Not found in gold of earth;
They worship truth and are aware
Of gold there is no dearth."
Black Mara roared, "I hate good men—
They always spoil my plan!
They have a god that teaches them
The brotherhood of man."

As Mara sneered the voice replied,
"Your god you now may prove.
But if he fails to answer you,
Beware and *do not move."*
Black Mara chanted magic words
Known only to this knave.
As he controlled the netherworld,
This power made him brave.

The voice spoke low to Squeaky Voice,
Who trembled as he heard,
"To conquer fear, perceive the light—
It holds our magic word."
Then Squeaky felt within his heart
The silence of the spheres;
The light of truth surrounded him,
Dissolving all his fears.

As Mara chanted lightning flashed,
And through the thunder roar,
Bright green, electric eyes appeared—
A hundred million score.
These eyes had tails of lightning flame.
They hissed through solar space.
Black Mara smelled sulfuric fumes
That clung around his face.

Then closer came these eyes of green
With tails of flaming light.
The voice cried out, "Call on your god
To stay their lightning might!"
Black Mara scoffed, "They can't hurt me—
I'm clothed in finest mail.
I fear no god, no man, nor you:
*My power* will prevail."

The lightning eyes now challenged him
With fervent, melting heat;
Black Mara's armor mail dissolved,
From helmet to his feet.
He rose and stood beside his chair—
His armor was no more.
Where had his earthly garments gone?
Where was his nether corps?

Then Squeaky saw a jet black robe
Drop over Mara's head.
The voice told him, "Your test proceeds
With souls whom you misled."
Young Squeaky thought about the voice
And Mara's coming test;
And Squeaky knew, the voice of light
Its truth would manifest.

## THE MAGIC LAMP

Young Squeaky Voice sat still and watched
  Black Mara look around.
The lightning eyes with tails of flame
  Dispersed without a sound.
"My god has power," Mara thought,
  "For I am still alive.
I have the greatest god of all!
  Through him I will survive."

Black Mara did not know the voice
  Could read his boasting thought
Until the voice began to speak.
  With sadness it was fraught.
"Your god of gold is not up here—
  You left your god below
With evil men who worship gold,
  The gift of earth god Go.

"The only thing you bring up here
  Is brother-love or hate;
We read your motive and your thoughts,
  And they decide your fate."
Black Mara jeered and called aloud,
  "My power none deny—
When men get greedy for my gold,
  Their souls I always buy."

The voice replied, "You hurt mankind
  With cunning, devil might;
You plan to steal our Magic Lamp,
  Which gives the world its light.
You could not bring old One Eye's oil—
  It has no power here.
Watch closely how we make *our* oil
  Above your earthly sphere.

"Our ether wave will now record
Men's thoughts from planet earth.
We keep these thoughts so men may see
What each has done from birth.
No man can hide his thoughts from light.
His motive is our clue—
Some men will cover evil thoughts
With deeds that seem quite true.

"These thoughts are graded in three groups.
When ready we transmute
These thoughts into our magic oil—
Its power none refute."
Black Mara laughed aloud and said,
"How can one see a thought—
Or catch one on an ether wave?
I'd like to see one caught!"

And then the curtain of the night
Revealed the crystal dome.
Black Mara cringed as once again
He saw King Sun's fine home.
He gazed until it disappeared;
Then Mara plainly saw
The Magic Lamp that gives its light
Through mighty cosmic law.

Beside the Magic Lamp he saw
A crystal cruet there,
Whose purity outshone the stars
Or cosmic jewels rare.
The voice spoke low, "We make true oil—
Look on the earth and see
Pure thoughts arise from kind, true hearts,
Wherever they may be."

Then Mara and young Squeaky Voice
Beheld a forest wild;
Within it stood a little girl—
A lost and frightened child.
Black Mara sneered as he watched her
Alone in darkened wood;

She shivered with the cold of night—
  She had no coat or hood.

Like older folk in mental fog,
  Confusion barred her way.
And Mara mocked at her sweet faith
  When she knelt down to pray.
The voice then said, "Such thoughts of faith
  Will benefit mankind;
The oil we make from her sweet faith
  Is very hard to find.

"We have her oil of faith, and now
  Our light transmutes again
The thoughts of brotherhood as they
  Arise from honest men."
Black Mara glared as one man said,
  "We come to plan for peace.
When we can purge our hearts of fear,
  This war of greed will cease."

"All men are greedy," Mara snarled.
  "Ah, no!" the voice replied.
"We make our oil from thoughts, not words,
  As words can be denied."
Then Mara saw two fine, young boys;
  They had a war to fight.
"Those boys are fighting," Mara jeered.
  "Their thoughts will not make light."

The voice replied, "Their motive will
  Make light that you can't see.
They fight *your* evil war, but their
  *Soul-light* will set them free.
We have enough of fine, pure oil
  To try some out for you.
Just watch the cruet fill the lamp,
  And see what it will do."

The cruet filled the Magic Lamp;
  The lamp began to burn;
Sweet manna fell upon the earth
  And filled a Crystal Churn.
This manna seemed to Squeaky Voice
  Like flakes of pure, white snow—
It floated from the Magic Lamp
  And drifted down below.

Sweet, kindly thoughts had brought to earth
  This manna, fresh and pure,
To feed all children who had faith,
  To help the weak endure.
The Dasher in the Crystal Churn
  Went flippity-flip-flop
And called aloud so all could hear,
  "Come help me—I can't stop!"

Poor children came from far and near.
  The strong ones brought the weak.
Some were so starved they could not walk;

And some, too ill to speak.
The weaker ones slept in the arms
Of gentle Mother Earth—
She healed them of their human ills
By giving them new birth.

And then the crippled ones could walk;
The blind could really see;
The deaf could hear the mute call out,
"My goodness—is this me?"
They danced around the Churn and called,
"What can we do for you?"
"Don't stop my Dasher," laughed the Churn.
"We have more work to do."

The Dasher answered with a flip,
"I've fed these kids before.
They love my butter, fresh and sweet,
And always yell for more.
I wondered why I worked so hard—
I really should have known:
Their thoughts have made sweet butter oil.
They reap what they have sown!"

The children saw the manna fall
And shouted in delight.
They peeked inside the Crystal Churn
All shining—clean and bright.
A baker worked inside the Churn,
His face a widened grin.

His cap hung on protrusive ear,
And flour was on his chin.

He winked at them and spooned his bread;
Then—presto!—in a trice,
They saw great pans of hot, sweet rolls
All crispy, brown, and nice.
"Now catch and eat these buttered rolls!"

The Crystal Churn called out.
The stronger children caught the rolls
With happy, joyous shout.

They fed the weaker children first,
With tender, loving care.
The Dasher called, "Come, bring your cups,
Our buttermilk to share."
The baker called, "Your kindly deeds
Make magic oil and bread.
Do one kind deed a day if you
Want hungry children fed.

"Sweet thoughts of faith, and good, kind deeds
Will make the manna fall.
Pray not for just yourself but pray
For food and health for all."
Deep silence reigned upon the earth.
The Churn now disappeared.
Young Squeaky sighed in glad content;
But Mara shrugged and sneered.

The crystal cruet then dissolved.
Another took its place.
This cruet formed into a pig
With selfish, greedy face.
Its color was a muddy gray;
Distended was its snout;
Its tongue, within its squealing mouth,
Was used as pouring spout.

The voice now spoke, "We make this oil
From thoughts of selfishness.
That willful boy who screams, 'No, no!'
Reveals his greediness."
Black Mara asked, "What ails that kid?"
The voice said, very sad,
"He has so much but will not share
With that small, crippled lad."

In glee Black Mara laughed and said,
"His parents are to blame;
They wrap his discipline in gifts.
He works them—like a game.
Bad, selfish kids make greedy men.
I'll keep my eye on him.
When he is grown, I'll buy his soul;
His greed will never dim."

The ether wave was making oil
As it went 'round and 'round;
It stopped above a women's group
Where color gray was found.
An honest woman soon arose
And then began to speak,
"Our starved and helpless call to you.
Your aid I come to seek."

A well-dressed woman answered her,
"We have our own to feed.
Another group will care for you

If you can prove your need.
To be well-groomed in these bad times
Is really quite a task;
Why should we women who keep homes
Neglect ourselves, I ask?

"I'm sure we do the best we can—
No need for such concern.
To close our business meeting now,
I move that we adjourn."
Black Mara laughed with evil mirth;
These women were his prey—
Their vanity shut out the light.
Each loved her selfish way.

The voice now said, "Look once again!"
Black Mara looked and saw
A group of men devising ways
To cheat within the law.
He knew this group of scheming men,
Puffed up with vain conceit,
Would go to church and give their alms
To cover their deceit.

Black Mara laughed until he saw
A flashing static ray
Go bouncing off the ether wave
To fill the cruet gray.
He thought to grasp the Magic Lamp,
Forgetting oil of thought.

The voice called out, "You must not move—
With danger it is fraught.

"You laugh when children disobey
And faith of men defile;
You gloat when men have greedy thoughts,
The products of your guile.
Since you enjoyed these selfish thoughts,
They now return to you;
Come, pour your oil of selfish greed
And see what it will do."

Black Mara thought, "I'll change this oil.
My plans I must revamp."
Then he poured oil from cruet-pig
And filled the Magic Lamp.
But when the lamp began to burn,
Black Mara changed his mind.
"Turn out that lamp!" he roared aloud.
"Its soot will make me blind.

"It's choking me and burns my throat—
My head spins 'round and 'round.
I cannot see, but I can hear
A dreadful, squeaking sound."
The oily soot had changed to bats.
Their mouse-squeaks filled the air.
Their mammal wings beat Mara's face.
They fastened in his hair.

Black Mara screamed, "Come, pull them off!"
The voice spoke, firm and clear,
"Although you call black-magic words,
You have no power here.
You came to steal the Magic Lamp,
Which gives its light to man.
These bats are greedy, selfish thoughts—
Enjoy them while you can."

Black Mara fumed, "Enjoy these bats!
Turn out that lamp, I say.
King Sun can keep his Magic Lamp,
But pull his bats away!"
The voice replied, "These bats dissolve
That you may now behold
Your greatest test—to prove your thoughts
Are black as devil-gold."

Black Mara said, "My thoughts are those
Enjoyed by most mankind;
Am I to blame for spineless men
Who have no thinking minds?"
As Mara sneered the voice replied,
"You have no soul or heart—
The vilest man upon the earth
Is your own counterpart."

Black Mara sat in cunning thought,
For he was not contrite.
He called upon his god of gold
To help him prove his might.
Could not his god dissolve the voice?
He planned just what to do;
His god of gold would guard him as
His course he would pursue.

"To get the Magic Lamp," he thought,
"The voice I must ensnare."
He did not see the dragon's head
Rise high above his chair.
But Squeaky saw the dragon move
Its ugly, crested head.
Its open mouth showed pointed teeth.
Its glassy eyes were red.

The dragon's wings were folded tight
Against Black Mara's back.
The legs upon the dragon-chair
Had mighty claws of black.
The arms upon this dragon-chair
Were made from furcate tail—
The left was black, the right was white,
Black Mara to assail.

Then Squeaky saw its red eyes blink,
Its right arm slowly move,
As Mara called, "I'm ready, voice!
My magic I will prove."
Young Squeaky shivered as he thought,
"This is the final test.
Will Mara or the voice win out?
Each one will do his best."

## BLACK MARA'S FINAL TEST

The dragon flashed its red-rimmed eyes
  As Mara clenched his fist.
Then louder Mara called the voice—
  How dare the voice resist!
"Come, come!" he called in greedy wrath.
  "I have no time to waste.
I've work to do upon the earth.
  I really must make haste."

From darkened silence spoke the voice,
  "Your sins are vile and bad.
Your evil thoughts have made your oil
  The blackest we have had."
The cruet-pig of selfish thoughts
  Dissolved in darkened space.
Another one stood by the lamp,
  With sneering devil-face.

Black Mara laughed in vain conceit,
  For he could plainly see
This devil-cruet looked like him—
  Satanic as could be.
The cruet's face had eyes of green
  That flashed in bitter scorn;
Its dark red forehead bulged into
  An evil handle-horn.

The handle-horn was sharp and smooth;
  The mouth, a cruel sneer
(This cruet was reflecting him
  With cunning, evil leer).
As Mara raged within himself,
  He grew an angry red;
Great scorpions with poison tails
  Came writhing from his head.

The voice then spoke, "Look down on earth!
Your own kind wait for you."
As Squeaky looked the cruet changed
To raging purple-blue.
The ether wave began to work.
Around the earth it went.
It stopped above a group of men
Where millions had been spent.

A scientist was speaking there
With energy and zeal,
"The secret of their atom bomb
We do not need to steal.
For I have here a soundless ray
That can destroy the earth—
Or heal the body ills of man
Before or after birth.

"This soundless, color ray of mine
Is called the *auric node.*
Dissolving planets, stars, or man,
This ray does not explode."
And as the warlords heard him talk,
Their leader said with greed,
"One million dollars we'll pay you—
By us it is decreed.

"We men will form a chosen group.
No others must survive.
Our chosen few will rule the world
To keep the peace alive."
"I thank you," said the scientist,
"For telling me your plan.
This auric node was made by me
To help my brother man.

"Of course, I have to watch its gauge,
For it is set so true
It can dissolve without a sound

A group as small as you."
The greedy leader called again,
"A billion will we give.
Then you and yours will be secure;
In wealth we all will live."

"I must explain my auric node,"
The scientist spoke low.
"All life vibrates to cosmic rays—
A fact you do not know.
The brain produces, while it thinks,
Its own, true, color ray.
My auric node can pick it up.
Its gauge is set that way.

"All evil men attract the black.
So then, without a sound,
This gauge upon my auric node
Will point where black is found.
Now watch my auric node detect—
Its power you must see.
Since they are made in pocket size,
I brought one here with me."

The warlords gave out frightened gasps,
Then ran in frantic fear.
Young Squeaky watched the warlords run
And grinned from ear to ear.
One warlord cried, "Such impudence!
Our gold he has defied.
He has more power than we have"—
A fact that none denied.

"Come, Mara!" said the voice to him.
"Pour oil just once again.
These warlords all belong to you—
The world's most evil men.
Their thoughts and yours are just alike—
Mass murder is your creed.
The Magic Lamp will prove to you
The horror of your greed."

Black Mara saw the cruet's face
Begin to leer at him.
The right chair-arm grew very warm.
And Mara's face grew grim.
"This is my chance to get the lamp!"
He thought in bitter scorn.
But when he felt his chair-arm move,
He grasped the cruet's horn.

But as he reached to seize the lamp,
Pretending to pour oil,
The right arm of his dragon-chair
Released its mighty coil.
It wrapped around Black Mara's waist
And held his arms so tight
That Mara could not break its hold
With all his magic might.

The dragon's red, satanic mouth
   Then bared its fangs of death;
Black Mara sickened from the stench
   Upon the dragon's breath.
He wildly called black-magic words
   Down to his nether plane;
He called upon his god of gold;
   But Mara called in vain.

The voice now said, "Just pour your oil.
   Too long have you delayed."
Black Mara's arm was then released,
   And quickly he obeyed.
As Mara filled the Magic Lamp,
   He gave his magic call;
The devil-cruet then dissolved
   Into a wailing wall.

Mad shrieks came from this wailing wall
   Of lost and evil souls.
Black Mara roared, "Such men as you
   My god of gold controls."
"We want release," the lost souls begged
   With frenzied, shrieking cries.
"Such weaklings," Mara taunted them,
   "I loathe and I despise.

"You sold yourselves to me for gold.
   In Hades you will stay—

I have too many souls like you
   To clutter up my way."
"Release us," begged the mad, lost souls.
   "No, no!" Black Mara cried.
"I have enough of souls like you—
   The world keeps me supplied."

These poor, lost souls, deformed by sin,
Now screamed like nether beasts;
They were the ones that She-Wolf saw
Attending Mara's feasts.
These lost souls begged for their release
From Mara's darkened night.
They did not know their sin held them
In Mara's evil might.

Black Mara jeered and taunted them,
Then laughed and called aloud,
"You surely do not want more gold—
And pockets in each shroud!"
The voice replied, "They need no gold.
From *you* they seek release.
Until these tortured souls find help,
Their cries will never cease."

Black Mara snarled, "They took my gold
And sold themselves to me.
It was their greed that blinded them—
Not one of them can see."
The voice then said, "Some blind folks see—
Through *love* they see mankind.
A loving heart has many eyes
Not found in thinking mind."

The lost souls screamed, "Some blind can see;
We want our sight—OUR SIGHT!
Come, Mara, give it back to us,
So we can see the light."
"No, no!" Black Mara screamed to them.
But lo! he was too late—
Their call for light released them from
The wailing wall of hate.

Black Mara saw them turn on him
And leave their beastly spore.
They groped for him with clawing hands;
They shrieked and screamed and swore.
He saw their sightless, red-rimmed eyes
And drooling mouths so weak.
Black Mara knew, upon his head,
Their vengeance they would wreak.

He cringed when they reached out for him
With cold and clammy hands.
He called to them, "Back to your wall!
I rule your nether lands."
The lost souls screamed, "Not any more!
We rule this testing space.
We are your hosts and represent
Each human creed and race.

"We have more power here than you.
Come, Mara, set us free.
We now outnumber living men.
The light we beg to see."
"You made a bargain," Mara cried.
"I sent you here to stay.

Why should you live again on earth?
With gold you'll have to pay!"

The lost souls screeched in evil glee.
They shook their binding chains.
"If we stay here," they called aloud,
"With us you will remain."
They snatched Black Mara from his chair
And called through evil jeers,
"We bind and hold you here with us
A hundred thousand years."

Black Mara cursed his god of gold;
Then loudly did he call,
"Come, voice, and send these fiendish souls
Back to their wailing wall."
The voice replied, "They asked for light;
Their begging you did spurn.
With greed you blinded them on earth;
Their sight you must return.

"You have your choice to stay with them—
They are your closest friends—
Or be the lowest man on earth.
On you it all depends.
If you decide to live on earth,
No matter where you go,
The vilest men will punish you
And hunt you as a foe.

"They will revile and laugh at you
And hound you from their door.
In vermin hovel you will live,
With slimy walls and floor.
The ceiling will be made of skulls
With sightless eyes that weep.
Their burning tears will waken you
When you could rest or sleep.

"These tears will sear your flesh with pain
And mark you with their scars:
You sinned against your fatherhood,
Entrusted to old Mars;
You disobeyed the cosmic law,
Beguiling honest youth;
You desecrated motherhood,
The fruit of light and truth.

"For eons you have preyed on man,
Defying GOD's great law—
To worship him in light and truth.
But *gold* was all you saw."
"I will return their gold to them,"
Called Mara, quite relieved.
The voice replied, "You have no gold—
Just souls whom you deceived.

"You said these souls belonged to you,
And based your claim on gold.
Because you prey on weaker men,

Your sins are manifold.
Remove your claim upon these souls—
They beg you for release.
Together you may all seek light,
The core of living peace.

"Do you not know the gold of earth
Is man's severest test?
Free choice must be for everyone,
To prove their worst or best."
Black Mara felt his power go.
He shook as with a chill.
Again the lost souls called to him,
Their voices sharp and shrill.

"Restore our sight, so we can see!
Release us to the voice!
He has a god that gives each man
The right to have free choice."
Black Mara cried, "Enough, enough!
Come, voice, and show me true
The path on earth that I must walk,
And what I have to do."

The voice replied, "One life on earth
Is far too short a span
For you to know our one true God
Rules nature gods and man.
To pay your debt, you now must live
Within your world of greed;
You cannot die or rest in sleep
Until these souls are freed.

"Your body structure will be pain,
Deformed by your past sin.
Through blinded eyes your heart must learn
To seek the light within.
When you and these lost souls seek light
Much more than earthly life,
Your eyes of heart will see the pyre
Of all your greed and strife.

"These lost souls now will go with you,
For doubly you must pay
The debt you owe to God and man—
There is no other way.
Deny no soul the right to choose
The path his feet will trod,
For each will form from his mistakes
His climbing stairs to God."

Then Squeaky heard that magic tone
And saw a wondrous light.
This light dissolved the netherworld,
The realm of Mara's might.
The Sapphire Stars breathed down on earth—
New souls were being born.
Out of the East, a maiden came
To bring the light of morn.

Then Squeaky saw in forest green
  Upon his earthly globe,
This maiden meet a handsome prince
  In royal purple robe.
And when she smiled upon the prince,
  Her blushes could be seen.
Young Squeaky grinned—she was his friend
  The lovely fairy queen.

*"Through mountain passes we must go*
*To seek this giant's trail.*
*To free those children is your test.*
*Let inner light prevail."*

## SQUEAKY VOICE SEES EONS AHEAD

"Awaken, Squeaky!" Grandad said.
"Black Mara's time is due.
Each thousand years he must report
To keep his record true."
"How will he come?" asked Squeaky Voice
As quickly he obeyed.
"You soon will see," old grandad said.
"We meet in Silver Glade."

But as they hurried toward the glade,
Awaiting in the wood
Young Squeaky saw the handsome prince
In royal cape and hood.
How Squeaky grinned when next he saw
The fairy queen so fair!
Spring flowers welcomed her approach
With perfume choice and rare.

She tiptoed right behind the prince
And covered his fine eyes.
"Guess who it is!" she gaily called.
He laughed in glad surprise.
The prince then took her hands in his,
Contented as could be.
"Our Magic Lamp is safe!" she said.
"All eyes of heart can see.

"I bring the news to Silver Glade:
Let all the earth rejoice!—
It is decreed to all mankind
The right to have free choice.
I hasten to good Mother Earth,
For she awaits my light.
Adieu until tomorrow morn,
My charming, sweet Prince Night!"

"Farewell, my queen, sweet Dawn," he said
With soft, caressing sigh.
Then Squeaky saw her blushes red
Suffuse the morning sky.
She smiled on Squeaky as she said
With simulated yawn,
"All children call me Fairy Queen.
My cosmic name is DAWN.

*"Sweet angel-fairies sing with me*
*Before King Sun's great throne.*
*Our rainbow is his music staff*
*Of cosmic color-tone."*

"Sweet angel-fairies sing with me
  Before King Sun's great throne.
Our rainbow is his music staff
  Of cosmic color-tone.
Our music notes are flower seeds
  That bloom for wise King Sun—
Their rainbow color-tones must prove
  All cosmic life is one."

The nature sprites beheld with joy
  The early-morning glow;
They gathered 'round good Mother Earth
  To welcome her son, Go.
For he had carried 'round the world
  Their heavy, golden cross—
Again it stood in Silver Glade
  On mound of flower-moss.

Young Go then greeted Mother Earth
  And gently said to her,
"Prepare this golden cross of man
  With frankincense and myrrh."
Young Go then said to lovely Dawn,
  "Awaken earthly man,
That each may see in his own cross
  The light of cosmic plan."

Then Dawn embraced good Mother Earth
  And whispered in her ear,
"The Holy Ones will manifest
  The light that will appear."
As Dawn approached the golden cross
  And touched the flower mound,
Gold-throated Easter lilies bloomed—
  For this was sacred ground.

Then Dawn bowed low to Mother Earth
  And faced the sleeping West.
"Awaken, Conscious Mind," she called.
  "This day is doubly blessed."
And then she welcomed with a smile
  Good Apas, brown and tall.
He touched the left arm of the cross
  And gave a magic call.

Good Apas said to Mother Earth
  Where quietly she stood,
"I christen thee—in living light—
  The Faith of Motherhood.
May faith flow from your nature-heart
  To heal all travail pain,
And may your soil produce for man
  Abundant fruit and grain."

Then Apas welcomed from the East
  Wise Vayu, god of air.
This bearded, yellow god bowed low.
  Clear vision he would share.
He touched the right arm of the cross,
  Then said to Mother Earth,

"May hope uplift the human soul—
Fatherhood of its birth.

"May hope give courage to the weak
And call within all men,
'Although you fall you must arise—
Again, again, again.
Your ship of soul will sail life's sea
If hope is calling you.
It is the anchor of your soul,
Your compass set and true.' "

Young Squeaky Voice was so intent
On hearing Vayu speak,
He did not see sweet Golden Fay
Until she touched his cheek.
She said, "Watch closely, Squeaky Voice,
And hearken to each word;
When I return, relate to me
All things both seen and heard."

Then Squeaky saw her fly away
To forest cool and dark;
She disappeared in dawning light,
Her crown a starry spark.
"What is her mission?" Squeaky thought.
"I wonder where she goes.
I think, from Grandad's knowing eyes,
Her mission he well knows."

Then from the North the fire god came.
The sky grew rosy red.
White Agni walked up to the cross
With firm and mighty tread.
He touched the top point of the cross,
Then all could plainly see
The top point change to circle-head.
The cross now formed a key.

Then Agni bowed to Mother Earth
And placed in her right hand
A tiny key of living flame
To purify her land.
He said to her, "Accept my gift,
This golden key of love.
Be wise as serpents of the light,
But harmless as the dove.

"May love unite all men in peace—
Of you they are a part—
The pulse-beat of true brotherhood
Comes from a loving heart."
Old grandad smiled at Squeaky Voice,
Then whispered in his ear,
"Your magic sight was earned through love,
Which casteth out all fear.

"Although you do not understand
These things you hear and see—
When each has been revealed to you,

Ethel Gesner

*Old grandad smiled when Squeaky Voice*
*Returned to sit with him—*
*Did not young Squeaky's love revive*
*His weary heart and limb?*

White Baw you then will be."
Then Squeaky saw the serpent-wheel.
Around the cross it spun,
Regenerating through the earth
The light of wise King Sun.

The nature gods and Mother Earth
Departed with their own.
But Squeaky stayed with Grandad Elf—
They heard the magic tone.
His school friends came to Silver Glade
On happy, marching feet.
They sang their praises to their Lord
In voices clear and sweet.

Young Squeaky grinned when Paul marched by
With Sally, Sue, and Joyce.
They called aloud, "Come march with us!"
To grinning Squeaky Voice.
As Squeaky marched along with them,
Quite loudly did he sing,
"We come to worship truth and light.
Accept these gifts we bring."

They placed sweet flowers and green palm
Around the cross of gold.
Each lit a candle from its light,
Its symbol to unfold.
Old grandad smiled when Squeaky Voice
Returned to sit with him—
Did not young Squeaky's love revive
His weary heart and limb?

He knew that he and Squeaky Voice
Would soon leave Silver Glade
And cross a land of giant beasts
Where brave men were afraid.
Young Squeaky had to earn the right
To hold the title *Baw*
And prove white-magic power was
The light in cosmic law.

The Silver Glade soon filled with folk.
A path led from the wood,
And on this path blind beggars came.
None had a cloak or hood.
Their leader and his men were bound
Together by a chain.
The chain was made from links of sin—
The earthly mark of Cain.

The leader cried, "I seek the voice!
Come, good folk, is he here?
Although my friends and I are blind,
I feel his presence near.
For eons I have sought for him
In courts of peace and strife,
But now my friends and I seek light
Much more than earthly life."

Then Squeaky saw sweet Golden Fay—
   She was the beggars' guide.
She led the beggars to the light,
   Which they had all denied.
Young Squeaky knew, as he sat still
   And watched sweet Golden Fay,
Her gift of intuition was
   The guide he must obey.

As Squeaky heard the leader speak,
   He knew who had returned—
Black Mara and his men now sought
   The light that each had spurned.
Black Mara's blinded friends had been
   The warlords of the earth;
Their genocides must be redeemed
   That they might have new birth.

The beggars wailed; Black Mara called,
  "We come to seek the light!
We seek the voice—to know his name—
  And beg of him our sight."
Then all the waiting crowd beheld
  A rainbow arching high.
The heavens welcomed with glad song
  The glowing, morning sky.

Bright angel-fairies sweetly sang
  From sapphire stars above,
"Oh, come rejoice! Let all adore
  Our Holy Lord of Love."
Transcendent light rayed from the cross
  In colors bright and true—
A flashing play of indigo
  With yellow, jade, and blue.

And those who sought with loving hearts
   Saw standing in this light
A being with uplifted hands,
   In robe of shining white.
His radiance went forth to bless
   All souls now being born.
His aura filled the Silver Glade
   To bless this holy morn.

The being touched the beggars' eyes
   With quickened, healing rays.
Their eyes of heart now saw the light;
   They sobbed with joyous praise.
At last the being silenced them
   As slowly he did speak,
"Oh, children of awakened hearts,
   Behold—the light you seek!"

The crowd stood silent, in deep awe.
   Then Mara loudly cried,
"You are the voice—the voice I seek—
   The voice that I denied."
Black Mara cried from longing heart,
   Beseeching in his woe,
"I long to hear your name, O voice—
   Your name I do not know."

The warlord-beggars cried aloud
   Again, again, again,
"We all beseech your name—your name!
   How are you known to men?"
"MY NAME," the being answered them,
   "Is written in the hearts
Of those who love their brother man—
   They are my counterparts.

"I am the LIGHT in each of you;
   I am the TRUTH in man;
I am the WISDOM of your soul;
   I am the HOLY PLAN.
My father God and I are ONE
   In you—or Abraham;
I am the VOICE of God in ALL,
   For I am—THAT—I am."

"He is Jehovah!" one man called.
   "I fear his wrath and ire.
He drew Elijah up to him
   In chariot of fire."
Another said, "He's Jesus Christ,
   My Lord, who speaks to me.
Our Holy Mother smiles on him—
   Her radiance I see."

"He is my Buddha of great heart,"
   Then called an eager youth.
"He's Krishna!" spoke a shepherd maid,
   "Arrayed in light and truth."
An old man sobbed, "My Lao-tse!
   I've waited long for him.

I see him smile within my heart—
  My outer eyes are dim."

Deep silence reigned in Silver Glade.
  Rare perfume filled the air.
All souls had recognized in him
  Their MASTER, standing there.
But Squeaky saw the rising sun
  Come forth in cosmic morn—
It was the Magic Lamp of light,
  In manifested form.

Old grandad said, "To be a Baw
  Your test has now begun."
Then Squeaky saw through magic sight
  The battle to be won.
He saw fierce giants wildly ride
  Through burning, desert sand
To pillage wealthy caravans
  That sought the holy land.

When Squeaky saw the giants' camp,
  He trembled in despair—
Their giant leader, Seven Head,
  Held captive children there.
"Those children weep," young Squeaky sighed.
  Old grandad gently said,
"You must outwit this giant beast.
  His name is Seven Head.

"Through mountain passes we must go
  To seek this giant's trail.
To free those children is your test.
  Let inner light prevail.
To be the White Baw of us elves,
  Come prove your magic sight—
Use secrets taught you from within
  The MAGIC LAMP of LIGHT."

*The Magic Lamp*

Designed by Mary Louise Crocker, Bonnie Irvine, and Janet Trone
Composed by Janet Trone
in Palatino® typeface
on a Macintosh® Plus computer
using Microsoft® Word software
Output by MacTypeNet™, Farmington Hills, Michigan,
on a Linotronic® 300 imagesetter
Color photographic reproduction work by G. P. Color, Los Angeles, California
Retouching by Mary Movradinov
Color separation by Spectrum, Inc., Golden, Colorado
Printed by Arcata Graphics/Kingsport
on S. D. Warren's Lustro Dull paper
Bound by Arcata Graphics/Kingsport
in Kivar® 5 Marine Blue Homespun
with Multicolor® Antique Spring Green endsheets